The Three Investigators

"We investigate anything"

The Crimebusters series

Hot Wheels
Murder to Go
Rough Stuff
Funny Business
An Ear for Danger
Hollywood Horror
Reel Trouble
Shoot the Works
Foul Play
Long Shot
Fatal Error

The Three Investigators

Rough Stuff

Funny Business

This edition published in 1995 for
Parragon Book Service Limited
Units 13–17 Avonbridge Industrial Estate
Atlantic Road
Avonmouth, Bristol BS11 9QD
by Diamond Books
77–85 Fulham Palace Road
Hammersmith, London W6 8JB

First edition published 1992 for Parragon
Book Service Limited

Printed in England

Rough Stuff

First published in a single volume in paperback in
the USA in 1989 Random House, Inc
First published in paperback in 1990 in Armada

1

Flying High

THE CESSNA HUMMED IN THE LATE MORNING SUNshine. Below the little plane, California's rugged Sierra Nevada range spread in a vast green sea of pine trees.

Bob Andrews looked out the cockpit window, binoculars to his eyes. Next to him, his father was piloting the single-engine turboprop high above the granite mountaintops and emerald valleys.

"There's something down there," Bob announced. "Just crossing that meadow. Spot it?"

Pete Crenshaw elbowed Jupiter Jones and winked. They were sitting in passenger seats behind Mr. Andrews and Bob. They had been gazing out their windows too, taking turns with the one pair of binoculars as they watched the changing mountain peaks below.

"Hey, that's a girl," Pete told Bob solemnly. "A gorgeous babe. She's gonna wave up at you any minute."

"Next she'll want your phone number," Jupiter said, grinning.

"And wonder if you're busy tonight," Pete added.

"Are there movies in Diamond Lake, Mr. Andrews?" Jupe asked innocently. "I think Bob's going to be busy. Pete and I'll need something to do."

Mr. Andrews chuckled.

Bob lowered the binoculars. "Actually, it was a cougar." He turned to look back at his friends. He was handsome, with tousled blond hair, dark blue eyes, and a magnetic smile. Wherever he went, girls seemed to appear . . . and to head right for him. "Very funny, but I'm not the one who's got to get a cheerleader's permission when *I* want a vacation."

"So who does?" Pete replied airily, conveniently forgetting the long explanation his girlfriend, Kelly Madigan, had extracted from him back home in Rocky Beach.

Bob turned to Jupe. "And when *I'm* out with a girl," Bob told him, "I don't bore her to death explaining the structure of the atom."

Jupe lifted his double chin and glared. "She said she wanted to get down to basics!" he said hotly.

Mr. Andrews roared with laughter. Jupe turned red. It was only at that instant that Jupe realized what she had meant.

The three friends laughed loudly, although Jupiter's laughter was slightly embarrassed. For all his intelligence, girls were still a mystery to him.

Jupe stood up carefully. He did not exactly look like a rock star. He had a round face and straight black hair, and he wore a loose Foreign Legion fatigue shirt to hide his large waistline. Someday his constant dieting would pay off. Until then, "husky" was the way he liked to describe himself. It was more dignified than "fat."

The Cessna had a low ceiling. Jupe ducked and moved to the tail, where odds and ends of equipment were jumbled together.

"Jupe, what're you doing?" Pete asked.

"Looking for more binoculars," Jupe said. "I want to spot my own girl down there, one who already knows $E = mc^2$."

Once again hearty laughter filled the Cessna, and now Jupe laughed loudest of all. It was a good start for a summer weekend. The sun shone brightly. The sky was a clear, untroubled blue. And one, two, or maybe even three days of freedom stretched ahead of them, depending on how long Mr. Andrews' news story kept him at Diamond Lake.

Now that they were in the air, their jobs and responsibilities left behind in Rocky Beach, nothing could stop them. They were going to have fun in one of the most exclusive mountain resorts in California. Diamond Lake boasted a championship golf course, an Olympic-size swimming pool, tennis courts, saunas, a stable of horses, and catered campouts. The resort even provided a landing strip for the planes of the glittering celebrities and wealthy executives who regularly escaped there.

Jupe rummaged noisily among the gear at the back of the plane. "With binoculars, maybe I'll spot

Mr. Andrews' contact," Jupiter said jokingly as he picked up and discarded some mechanics' tools, an empty juice container, a battered Nerf ball, and other assorted junk. "What did you say his name was, Mr. Andrews?"

"I didn't say," Mr. Andrews responded immediately.

"Aha!" Jupiter said. "Your news source is a man. I said, '*his* name' and you answered. That's our first clue, guys!"

"Nonsense," Mr. Andrews said, but he smiled. Jupe was right.

"Come on, Dad," Bob urged. "Who is he? We won't tell anyone."

"Sorry." Mr. Andrews shook his head. He was a slender, good-natured man, a little under six feet, with big hands and feet. He was still a hair taller than his son, but probably not for long. He wore dark glasses, a Los Angeles Dodgers' baseball cap, and a navy blue Windbreaker with a half-dozen pencils sticking out of the breast pocket.

"What kind of story are you working on?" Pete asked. "Something about a super athlete? Somebody doing high-altitude training at Diamond Lake?" Pete, a natural athlete, was more into physical stuff than his friends. He was a tall, muscular guy whose strength had helped them out of many tight spots. "Hey, I know, a boxer! The state championship finals start next month!"

"You won't get even a hint from me. A reporter

must protect his news sources," Mr. Andrews reminded them.

"Oh, do we *know*!" Bob sighed. "Without confidential sources," he continued, repeating the words he'd heard many times, "a reporter sometimes can't get the whole story."

"And if a reporter names his sources," Pete ended the familiar refrain, "they all dry up!"

"We know how important secrecy is," Jupe assured Mr. Andrews, "and you can count on us not telling *anyone*!"

Mr. Andrews grinned. "You bet. You can't tell what you don't know!"

The three guys groaned. Mr. Andrews was tough. No wonder he was one of the top reporters for a major Los Angeles newspaper. There was no way he was going to reveal the story he was onto now.

At home the day before Bob had overheard him making arrangements to use one of the newspaper's small planes to fly to Diamond Lake on special assignment. Bob knew a hot tip was involved, but who, what, and why had eluded him.

"How'd I ever talk you into letting us come along?" Bob grumbled.

"Charm," Mr. Andrews said. "That same charm you turn on whenever there's a pretty girl within fifty feet." He shot his son a look of admiration, then said sternly, "And your sincere promise that you'd mind your own business. Remember, this is *not* a job for the Three Investigators."

The guys remembered. For years they had operated their own semiprofessional detective agency—semiprofessional because they were underage and worked without state licenses and couldn't charge a fee. Still, they could never resist a mystery. At seventeen, they had already solved many baffling cases, explained a lot of odd happenings, and even brought some crooks and thieves to justice.

"Hey, give us a break. We're on vacation!" Pete assured Mr. Andrews.

"R & R," Jupe agreed. "Rest and relaxation."

"No," Pete corrected, "rest and *recreation*."

Bob turned around and grinned at them. "And women!" he kidded.

Jupiter lobbed the Nerf ball across the cabin. It hit Bob in the face with a plop.

Pete shoved Bob back down in his seat and held him there while the smaller guy struggled and hooted.

"Hey, I didn't give up three days' pay for this kind of abuse," Bob managed to say, laughing.

So he could make the trip, Bob had taken time off from his gofer job at the Rock-Plus talent agency. Pete had left the old Studebaker sedan he was fixing up for resale in the able hands of Ty Cassey, who was Jupe's cousin and a crack auto mechanic. And Jupe had printed out the complete inventory of the Jones Salvage Yard—two copies. The salvage yard was a family business run by Jupe's Uncle Titus and Aunt Mathilda. Jupe had entered the yard's entire contents into his computer, but whenever his uncle or aunt tried to use it, they invariably erased the file.

With the money they'd saved from their summer work, the guys could afford cots in Mr. Andrews' hotel room and simple meals. Lying around the hotel pool was free, and they hoped to find other interesting entertainment for the same low price.

"Hey, fellows," Mr. Andrews said, "this is worth looking at. See that valley?" He nodded ahead into the distance.

Bob peered through the binoculars, then handed them back to Pete. Both guys leaned forward, continuing to watch.

"Might as well go down for a closer look," Mr. Andrews said. "We're almost at Diamond Lake."

The plane's nose dipped, the engine humming rhythmically.

Jupe gave up trying to find more binoculars and moved back to his seat behind Mr. Andrews. He looked ahead at the narrow green valley in the distance. It had tall, sheer granite walls and seemed to run almost straight north and south. At its southern end a cliff ran east and west for some miles to either side. A silvery waterfall cascaded down the cliff and out the valley.

"That's an awesome sight," Jupe agreed.

"What's that valley called?" Bob wondered.

"Wish I knew," Mr. Andrews said. "It's a beaut. Look on ahead. There's Diamond Lake, another forty or so nautical miles north of us."

Mercury and blue, almost round, Diamond Lake

glistened like an alpine gem in the sunshine. Tiny ant-size buildings clustered on one edge. A white concrete road ribboned through the mountains and around its shore.

Bob whistled as he gazed at it. "All *right!*"

"And we'll be just in time for lunch!" Jupe exclaimed.

"Now you're talking," Pete agreed.

Just then, the Cessna gave a little jerk. Or at least Jupiter thought so. It was barely noticeable. . . .

"Did you feel . . ." Jupe began.

Then time seemed to stop.

The three guys looked at one another and then forward to the Cessna's sole engine.

The comforting hum of the motor was gone. The engine was silent.

"Mr. Andrews . . ."

His hands were already speeding over the controls. He had had his pilot's license for two years, had flown the newspaper's planes many times, had never had a problem.

He flipped switches, checked gauges, and stared for a moment, stunned, as nothing responded. The needles lay flat, didn't move. Numbers didn't register. Altitude, air speed, fuel . . .

"The electrical system's out!" Bob realized.

"The engine?" Jupe asked, although he knew the answer.

"Dead," Mr. Andrews said. "We've got to head down before we stall out!"

2

A Real Downer

THE CESSNA STREAKED THROUGH THE SKY, THE engine silent. The air whistled and groaned around it. Mr. Andrews grabbed the microphone from the instrument panel and pushed the button.

"Mayday! Mayday!" His voice was calm but urgent. "This is Cessna November 3638 Papa. Lost our engine. Going down. Position is 047 radial of Bakersfield VOR at 75DME!"

Mr. Andrews thrust the mike at Bob and returned to the stick.

Bob pushed the button and repeated. "This is Cessna November—"

Mr. Andrews suddenly paled. "Forget it, Bob," he interrupted. "It's too late."

"What?" Bob asked, confused.

"The electrical system's gone," Jupe said, "so there's no radio."

"We've got an emergency locator beacon," Bob remembered. "It goes on automatically if the airplane crashes."

"I'd rather not crash, thank you," Jupe said, his heart pounding. "If we can just reach the ground safely. . . ."

"Yes," Bob and Pete breathed.

Silently they tightened their seat belts.

"What's the stall speed?" Jupe asked.

"About eighty miles per hour, this plane," Mr. Andrews said tersely.

"What does that mean?" Pete asked worriedly.

"If we go too slow, we stall," Jupiter said. Jupe's round face was pinched. "We've got to keep the nose pointed down. So gravity'll pull us faster than eighty."

"If we stall," Bob said grimly, "we drop like a rock."

"Why don't you sit on the nose, Jupe?" Pete tried to joke.

The guys smiled wanly but tension crackled in the small cabin. The plane's nose was aimed at the granite peaks below. The craft seemed as fragile as a toy. If it hit one of those mountaintops, it would smash into matchsticks. And they would too!

Fear knotted Jupiter's stomach and doused him with sweat.

Pete flexed his hands, cracking his knuckles. His muscles were so tight he wanted to jump out of his skin.

Bob swallowed, trying to breathe evenly. He promised himself he'd never again tease Jupe about his weight, or Pete about Kelly, if only they'd all survive. . . .

"Where are we headed?" Bob asked. The words came out with a strangled sound.

"That meadow," Mr. Andrews said. It was big, located east of the valley they'd seen earlier.

"How long?" Jupe said.

"Three minutes. About."

The guys stared frozen out the windows. They couldn't stop watching as they sliced downward through the air. The trees and granite below grew bigger and bigger. The long cliff north of the meadow got taller, whiter, towering.

Bob thought about his mom. It would be terrible if she read about the crash in the papers. Dad and him *dead*.

The closer the plane got to the ground, the faster it seemed to go—rocketing at top speed into disaster!

"Duck down!" Mr. Andrews snapped. "Wrap your arms over your heads!"

"Dad—"

"You too, Bob. No heroics."

Bob leaned over and put his arms around his head. "At least we've got landing gear," he muttered, trying to reassure himself and the others. "The wheels are nonretractable."

No one mentioned brakes. With the electrical system out, the brakes were unusable.

The rush of air around the plane grew louder.

This is it! Bob thought miserably.

The Cessna hit the earth.

Bob and the other guys slammed forward against their seat belts, then rammed back into their seats. Sharp pain shot red and white sparks behind Bob's eyes.

The plane leaped back up into the air and crashed down again with teeth-rattling force. It jerked all of them like puppets back and forth against their seat belts. The Cessna jumped up again.

"Hold on!" Mr. Andrews shouted.

The plane hit the ground a third time. It shuddered, bounced, and groaned. But it didn't rise again. It hurtled forward like a cannonball out of control.

Bob held on to his seat belt, trying to keep his head low as the terrific ground speed pitched him back into his seat. His insides felt like Jell-O. All of them were still alive, but for how much longer?

Suddenly there was the ear-splitting scream of metal wrenched from metal.

Bob, his dad, and the other guys slammed forward and lurched back. Their heads struck the side walls. Books and papers flew through the air. Electrical cords and pieces of equipment sailed past. Something hit Bob's arm. Pain registered in his brain. He could hardly breathe as the plane spun and wrenched from side to side.

And then there was silence. A stunned silence. The Cessna had stopped.

Slowly Bob raised his head.

"Dad!"

Mr. Andrews was slumped forward against the instrument panel.

Bob shook his father's shoulder. "Dad! Are you okay?" His father didn't move.

"Let's get him out of here!" Pete ordered as he stepped between the two front seats.

Quickly Bob unplugged Mr. Andrews' earphones. Pete released the unconscious pilot's seat belt. There was blood on Mr. Andrews' forehead, and a huge bruise that was already turning an angry red.

Bob stumbled out the door with Pete behind him, and ran around to the other side of the plane. He was okay, and Pete and Jupe seemed okay, but his father was hurt! He yanked open the pilot's door. *Dad's still breathing!* he told himself eagerly.

Pete appeared at Bob's side. He scooped Mr. Andrews up into his strong arms, cradling him like a baby. Pete didn't have time to dwell on his own minor aches and pains. Mr. Andrews needed his help.

"Where's Jupiter?" Pete called to Bob as he ran toward the shelter of tall boulders. Bob ran alongside him, watching his dad with eagle eyes.

"Here." Jupe's voice was faint, groggy. He was still in the plane, and he felt lousy. Slowly he moved his arms and legs, testing them. They seemed to work okay. . . .

"Get out of there, you idiot!" Pete bellowed at him as he ran around some tall granite boulders.

Pete laid Mr. Andrews down on a patch of grass.

Bob leaned over him, feeling for the pulse in his neck. "Dad, can you hear me?" he said. "Dad?"

Pete raced back to Jupe.

"I'm coming," Jupe mumbled. He glared grumpily out the door at Pete.

"The fuel tanks!" Pete snapped, grabbing Jupe's arm.

Jupe's eyes opened wide. "The fuel tanks!" he repeated in horror. The engine would be red hot, and if the fuel tanks had ruptured . . . gas could leak onto it and ignite!

Jupe fell out the side door and scrambled to his feet. He didn't have time to test his body anymore. Either it would work or it wouldn't! He stumbled and began to run behind Pete. They headed toward the high boulders that shielded Mr. Andrews and Bob from the plane.

Jupe fell next to Mr. Andrews, panting, his round face glistening with sweat. Pete crouched beside Jupe.

Now they waited for the explosion, for the heat and oily stench of sudden fire.

Bob had taken off his denim jacket, rolled it up, and slipped it under his father's head. "His pulse is steady," he said, and looked at his two friends.

Jupe nodded. "Let's hope he's just been knocked out temporarily."

"He's a tough guy," Pete reminded Bob. He took off his own jacket, covered Mr. Andrews, and stood up. He stretched and swung his arms, then squatted back down to wait for the plane to explode . . . or the engine to cool. His back hurt from being thrown backward in his seat so many times, and his chest hurt a little from the seat belt, but he told himself it wasn't much worse than a workout at the gym.

Mr. Andrews moaned.

"Dad?" Bob said at once. "Wake up, Dad."

"Can you hear us, Mr. Andrews?" Jupe said.

Mr. Andrews' eyes opened and he looked at Bob.

Bob grinned happily. "Great landing, Dad."

"A real three-pointer," Jupe agreed.

"So, when do we start flying lessons?" Pete wanted to know.

Mr. Andrews smiled painfully. "You all okay?"

"Better than the plane, anyway," Jupe said.

Mr. Andrews started to sit up. Bob pushed him down.

"The plane!" Mr. Andrews exclaimed. "Did the wing come off?"

"The wing?"

The guys stood and looked around the boulders at the scene of destruction. A long earthen scar marked the plane's progress across the flower-filled meadow. Shattered saplings stood upright in the sunshine, their tops severed by the Cessna's wings. One four-foot propeller blade had snapped. It lay in pieces a hundred feet away. Two of the landing wheels rested on their sides in the Cessna's tracks. And the starboard wing was ripped off, caught in the claw of the rock formation that had finally stopped the Cessna. Without its wing the plane would not fly out of the meadow—or anywhere.

"Wow," Bob said.

"That *was* some landing," Pete said with respect.

"And all I've got is a few bruises," Jupe said with wonder.

"Where's my cap?" Mr. Andrews said. Ignoring them, he grabbed the side of the boulder and pulled himself up.

"Dad!"

"Mr. Andrews!"

Mr. Andrews leaned against the boulder and held his head. He smiled ruefully. "Bit of a headache."

"You'd better sit down!" Bob insisted.

"No way, fella," Mr. Andrews said. "I've got to check out that plane."

"But the engine . . ." Pete began.

"Might explode?" asked Mr. Andrews. "If it hasn't yet, it probably won't." He turned toward the Cessna. Gingerly he put one foot in front of the other. "Not so bad," he muttered.

Bob grabbed one arm to support him, and Pete grabbed the other.

"Anyone ever tell you you're pigheaded?" Bob asked his dad.

"My city editor," Mr. Andrews replied cheerfully. "All the time." But he let the guys help him.

Jupe walked alongside them. When they got to the wrecked Cessna, Bob reached across the pilot's seat and picked up Mr. Andrews' sunglasses and Dodgers cap. Mr. Andrews tucked the sunglasses into the pocket of his blue Windbreaker. He turned the cap in his hands and tried it on the back of his head, away from the bump on his forehead. He adjusted it and grinned. He could wear it.

Now they surveyed the big downward-sloping meadow and the thick forest that surrounded it. In the distance on three sides of them, high granite peaks gleamed in the sun. Behind them a long cliff rose two hundred feet and extended into the forest on either side of the meadow. The tall cliff blocked the peaks to the north from view.

There was no sign of civilization. Diamond Lake was thirty or forty miles away and out of sight somewhere on the other side of the cliff.

Bob studied the terrain. At any other time, he would have thought how great looking it was. The sharp, dramatic peaks stood over valleys covered with such thick trees that you couldn't see the ground. But now all he could think about was that they were alone. They were downed in a remote mountain meadow without water, food, radio, transportation, or camping gear.

"Well, fellows," Mr. Andrews said tiredly as if he could hear Bob's thoughts, "how are your wilderness skills?"

3

California Tough

"JUST HOW COLD WILL IT GET?" BOB ASKED HIS father. They were sitting outside in the warm sunshine while Pete and Jupe searched the plane for a medical kit and a container to hold water.

"Not bad," Mr. Andrews replied. "August is early for a freeze. Probably won't drop below forty tonight."

"Forty!" Bob's eyebrows shot up. "That's cold!"

"That's my boy." Mr. Andrews smiled. "A rough Californian through and through."

"Hey, this is the land of nonstop rays," Pete said as he hopped down from the plane and trotted toward them. He was holding a flat metal box in one hand.

"We're genetically programmed for warmth!" Bob agreed.

Pete's stomach rumbled loudly. "We're also programmed to eat. I was looking forward to lunch in Diamond Lake," he said ruefully. "A *big* lunch."

Bob and Mr. Andrews nodded. They were hungry too.

"At least it's good for Jupe's diet," Bob said.

"Whatever new one he's trying today!" Pete laughed.

Mr. Andrews looked optimistic. "Well, with a little luck we'll be out of here soon. Somebody'll hear our Mayday beacon. It's broadcasting right now on 121.5 megahertz."

"You sure it's on?" Pete asked, suddenly nervous.

"It's automatic," Mr. Andrews assured him. "Operates on a battery. It turns itself on at impact. I've heard stories that if you just accidentally drop one, there's sometimes enough G-force to start it going."

Mr. Andrews nodded at a faint white trail high in the blue sky above them. "That jet may be too far away to see us, but it can hear our SOS signal."

Bob glanced at the faraway craft, then grinned at his father. He was relieved. They were in a bad spot, but his dad was talking so easily that he had to be feeling better. And they were going to be rescued.

"What'd you find, Pete?" he asked his friend.

"An emergency kit. Dusty, but all ours."

"Dynamite!" Bob said.

They opened the metal box. Inside were aspirin, biodegradable soap, bandages, mosquito repellent, skin antibiotic, iodine pills to purify water, a box of wooden kitchen matches, and six lightweight "space blankets" of a shiny material so thin that each folded compactly into a three-by-five-inch square.

"Matches!" Bob said triumphantly.

"Iodine pills," Mr. Andrews said. "Now we'll have safe drinking water."

"This looks like the stuff astronauts wear," Pete said as he shook out a space blanket. He tucked the edge into the neck of his T-shirt like a cape. "Hey, guys, look. Think I can pass for a rock star?"

With supplies from the emergency kit, Bob cleaned and bandaged Mr. Andrews' forehead. The wound was superficial, but the bruised flesh had turned into a large, purple bump.

Bob studied the swollen flesh. "You'd better take it easy, Dad. Head wounds can be tricky. If you get dizzy, sit down . . ."

"I'm glad I sent you to those Red Cross classes," Mr. Andrews said cheerfully.

"Me, too."

Pete, his cape neatly folded again, ranged along the edge of the meadow gathering dry wood. He stacked it by the boulders where they had first found shelter. If they needed a fire, they'd build it away from the plane—and the fuel.

Jupe had been searching the Cessna for a water container.

"Hey, guys!" he shouted. His voice sounded worried. "We've got a problem!"

Bob and Pete ran to the plane, Mr. Andrews close behind.

"It's the Mayday beacon," Jupe announced grimly. "It's not working."

"Show me," Mr. Andrews said curtly.

Jupe had opened the beacon box. "A little red light on the outside's supposed to flicker. That's how you know it's signaling. The wiring and connections are okay. The only thing that could be wrong is the battery. Looks to me like it's dead."

"Dead?" Bob echoed miserably.

"Then it hasn't sent *any* help signal?" Pete asked. His eyes were wide with shock.

"I don't see how it could've," Jupe said.

"Oh, boy," Pete said. He opened and closed his fists. He could feel his heart pumping with adrenaline. This was terrible!

"First the electrical system," Bob said, shaking his head. "Now this!" He felt a little sick.

"We're jinxed," Pete said.

"Electrical systems go out sometimes," Mr. Andrews said. "It's rare, but it happens. Faulty connections, for instance. And batteries sometimes don't get checked when they should. Which means they don't get replaced."

"This is the pits," Pete muttered.

There was nothing they could do. They climbed out of the plane. The afternoon wind whistled through the pines rimming the big grassy meadow. Behind them the cliff rose in easy levels toward the crystal-blue sky.

"Paradise," Bob said, and shook his head.

"Yes, it could fool you," Mr. Andrews said.

"Not me," Jupe said. "Poisonous snakes, avalanches, sharp precipices, forest fires, lightning, hungry carnivores, poisonous berries. Just to name a few problems." Jupe had never trusted the outdoors.

"Wait a minute," Bob said, his voice hopeful. "What about your contact in Diamond Lake, Dad? He'll think something's wrong when we don't show up on time."

"He didn't know you guys were coming," Mr. Andrews said. "Because I didn't know the last time I spoke to him. When I don't show up, he might call the paper. Otherwise it'll be three days before anyone back home starts to worry about us."

"Terrific," Pete muttered.

"Okay, Pete, you've gone camping before, right?" Mr. Andrews said. "What should we do first?"

"First we see what we've got," Pete said, rallying. "All I have is what I'm wearing." He was dressed in his usual jeans and tennis shoes. Today's T-shirt was black and had the name of the rock group Pink Floyd in big gold letters on the front. "Plus I've got a jacket, a pocketknife, and some extra clothes in my suitcase. What about you guys?"

"I guess I'm in the same boat," Bob said. His jeans were Calvin Klein, and his T-shirt had a Banana Republic Minister of Culture emblem. "But no knife."

"Me neither," Mr. Andrews said. He had on jeans, a shirt, his jacket and cap.

"Yeah, I wish I'd known I'd need backpacking gear," Jupe said. He sighed. "Three days aren't so bad, even though we have to deal with the elements and not much to eat—"

"Hold on!" Bob said. "What's this 'not much to eat'

stuff? You're holding out on us, otherwise you'd say *nothing to eat!* You've got food!"

Jupe's round face flushed. "Well, not exactly."

"Food!" Pete exclaimed. "Give!"

"You don't have to short out your circuits!" Jupe said indignantly. "All you have to do is ask . . ."

"We're asking!" Pete said.

"I could stand a bite," Mr. Andrews admitted.

Jupiter shrugged. "Okay, but this won't turn you on." He disappeared into the plane.

"Hey, what's taking you so long?" Pete demanded. "You got a microwave in there?"

Jupiter reappeared with his duffel. It was bright red with white stripes encircling each end and the words I CAME FROM PIZZA HEAVEN, INC. printed on the sides. He pulled out a plastic bag of popcorn, a bag of unpopped kernels, and a variety of candy bars.

"Let me at it!" Pete announced. His stomach growled. "Give!"

"This is a diet?" Bob asked, incredulous. "And why aren't you starving too? I bet you've got a stash in your pocket!"

"I am on a popcorn diet," Jupe said stiffly, drawing himself up to his full portly height of five feet eight and three-quarter inches. "I must eat a cup of popcorn every two hours. I have just completed my scheduled snack." Ceremoniously he reached into two enormous shirt pockets and brought out three more little bags of popped popcorn, about a cup each. He gave them to Pete, Bob, and Mr. Andrews. "It's all yours."

"And the candy bars?" Pete said, diving into his popcorn.

"Help yourself," Jupe said archly.

"Some diet," Bob said. "Candy bars." He ate eagerly. He was definitely feeling better.

"It's better than some of his other diets," Pete said. "Remember the grapefruit and prunes?"

"Or the pancakes and French fries?" Bob said.

"How about that canned liquid stuff that smelled like gasoline?" Pete said.

He and Bob groaned, remembering.

"I must admit," Jupe said thoughtfully, "that the carboliquid was particularly ineffective." He smiled. "This diet, however, appears to have more salutary results."

"What'd he say?" Pete asked Bob.

"He's cautiously optimistic," Bob replied.

Pete stared questioningly at Mr. Andrews.

Mr. Andrews grinned. "Jupe thinks he's maybe losing some weight." He put some popcorn in his mouth.

Pete shook his head. "Jupe, why don't you exercise? Go back to your judo class." He flexed his arms and twisted his athletic torso. "You'll lose weight and feel great."

Jupe leaned against the plane, looking pale. "Whenever I feel like exercising," he said, closing his eyes, "I lie down and wait for the urge to go away."

They laughed. Jupiter opened his eyes and smiled broadly. He had flexed, exercised, and trained his brain into a finely tuned instrument. That was good enough for him.

"Thanks for the food, Jupe," Mr. Andrews said. "Divide it up for three days. But remember, we could be here longer."

"Let's look for help," Pete said. "Maybe there's a ranger cabin around here. Or a campground or road. We need water, no matter what. When I was gathering wood, I heard a stream running over there somewhere." He pointed southwest. "And campgrounds are usually on streams."

"You can use this to carry water," Jupe said. He reached into the Cessna and retrieved a two-quart plastic bottle that had once held orange juice.

"Good," Pete said, and handed it to Bob. "Wash it out with the soap, fill it with clean water, and drop in the iodine pills to make it safe to drink."

Bob took the water bottle from Pete. "No problem. What're you going to do?"

"I saw a trail in the woods south of here. It's probably an animal path. But who knows?"

"Good thinking, Pete," Mr. Andrews said. "I'll climb the cliff." He nodded toward the granite wall that ran along the northern edge of the meadow. The cliff rose in easy-to-climb mounds. "From the top, I ought to be able to see a long way. Maybe I'll spot a fire lookout."

"You feel okay enough to do that, Dad?" Bob asked.

"Like you said, son. No problem."

Now Mr. Andrews, Pete, and Bob looked expectantly at Jupiter.

"We-ell," Jupe said. "Guess I'll stick around here. Just in case we're rescued."

"We need more wood," Pete told him. "*Wet* wood, so we can build a big, smoky signal fire. And then you could get some shirts out of our suitcases. Climb three or four trees and tie the shirts to the top like flags."

As Pete talked, Jupiter seemed to wilt with exhaustion. Bob had a sudden image of their overweight friend perched on the top of a pine tree, like an oversize Christmas ornament. He cracked up.

"And after that," Pete continued cheerfully, "roll some rocks into the middle of the meadow and spell out SOS real big in case a plane flies low enough to read it."

Jupiter groaned. "You want me to build a log cabin while I'm at it?" The others laughed.

"All right, all right," Jupe said. "I'll pick up some wet wood."

"Lots!" Pete said, and he and Bob took off.

"Remember to use landmarks!" Mr. Andrews called after them. "It's easy to get turned around in the forest!"

Bob and Pete separated at the meadow's edge. Bob plunged southwest into the pine forest, heading toward the faint sound of rushing water. Pete disappeared southeast into the forest on the animal trail he had discovered earlier.

Remembering his father's words, Bob carefully

watched where he was going. He passed an unusual triple pine—three trees that had begun growing together as saplings and now formed a single thick trunk of three irregular cylinders. Later he passed a flat boulder with deep bowl-like indentations. It looked as if ancient Indians had ground nuts into flour there with stone pestles. He saw other landmarks and committed the sequence to memory, until at last he found an animal path. He followed the path toward the sound of the stream. The rushing water grew louder and louder.

And then he saw it, a shallow river about twenty feet wide. The water pounded over rocks, twigs, and a pebble-strewn bed. Sunlight sparkled on parts of it, while other parts, deep in the shadows of trees, were almost black. The stream was crystal clear and looked perfect for drinking.

Bob washed out the orange juice bottle with the biodegradable soap that had been in the plane's emergency kit. Then he rinsed it, filled it with water, and dropped in the iodine pills.

He stood and looked up and down the stream. His next assignment was to find help—a campground would be most likely. Upstream or down?

He thought about the valley they had seen from the plane. He knew it was west of the meadow, and that it had had a stream running through it. This could be the same stream. If his calculations were right, the valley would be due north of where he now stood. It was very likely that such a beautiful valley would have a public campground in it.

Bob headed upstream, sometimes able to walk along the water and at other times going inland to circle past boulders, prickly brush, or marshes. As he moved, the sound of rushing water grew louder.

At last he stepped around a stand of red manzanita trees and out to an open space where the stream swept down over rapids. Spilling into the rapids was a long, sheer waterfall. The sight was extraordinary. The churning water roared like a million bumblebees.

Bob breathed in the misty air. He gazed up at the waterfall and up, up at the dramatic cliff that rose high above it on either side. The falls had cut a deep notch in the rockface.

If this was the waterfall Bob had seen from the plane, then the valley should be just beyond the cliff. He needed to climb that wall of rock. The question was where to start.

Bob studied the granite face and spotted a place where the stone separated, forming a foothold. He put down his water bottle, stepped carefully over a huge pile of rock debris, and started up the cliff. Stones spun away from his feet. He climbed slowly, gripping little outcroppings and tree roots.

And then it happened.

From above, a few small rocks pelted down on his head. He heard a rumble.

He looked up. A big rock was coming down to his right, gathering debris with it. A landslide was racing down to crush him!

4

Double Trouble

ON THE CLIFF ABOVE BOB, THE LANDSLIDE GAINED momentum. He couldn't go back, he'd be smack in the path of the rock. Fear tightened his throat. No time for thinking. Time to move!

He scrambled left, hugging the face of the cliff. Sweat ran down his forehead and burned his eyes. Rock dust clogged his nose.

He frantically edged sideways.

The rumble grew.

The landslide exploded past him. Tiny stones stung his skin like needles.

The big slide dumped onto the loose rocks at the base. That enormous pile was talus, Bob realized, formed by centuries of landslides just like this one. The cliff was unstable. Anything could have set it off—a mountain lion, an earth tremor, or just a rock that erosion had finally worked loose. The cliff wasn't safe for climbing!

Bob's heart pounded. He closed his eyes, still feeling the terror of the near miss.

But he couldn't stay there forever.

He opened his eyes and looked around. What should he do? Go up? Go back down?

And then he saw a strange sight. Handholds—or footholds. No, both! And they were carved! No natural phenomenon could have created such a perfect set of individual shelves for the feet and curved grips for the fingers.

Still a little shaky, Bob stepped from the crack to which he clung and into the security of the handholds and footholds. Now he could see there were many of them. They extended in a tidy but dangerous path, angling upward to the left on the face of the sheer cliff. They were carved in what appeared to be a stable section, perhaps by the same long-ago Indians who had ground bowls into the granite boulder he'd passed earlier.

Bob looked at his watch. It was getting late. The others would be waiting for him.

He crawled on, staying in the handholds and footholds as he moved upward along the cliff. He reached the notch above the falls and continued around the corner into a deep, eroded channel, moving upstream. The cold spray from the waterfall beneath him misted the air.

And there it was opening up before him—the beautiful valley they had seen from the air. It was forested and wide in places, and extended farther than he could see. The cliffs that rimmed it were pale granite and sparkled in the sun. The stream flowing through its center was flat and peaceful, far different from the torrent that spilled over the waterfall and rapids. But the campground he had hoped to find wasn't there.

The wind was blowing from the north. It carried the stench of sulfur, which meant there were probably hot springs in the valley. For a moment Bob's eyes stung, irritated. He turned his head away, and then back again for a final view.

It seemed very long ago that he, Jupe, Pete, and his father had spotted the valley from the air. So much had happened since then. They were lucky to be alive. If it hadn't been for his father's sharp piloting when the electrical system went out . . .

He stopped the thought and turned away to follow the handholds and footholds back down the channel, around the corner, and onto the cliff face. He passed the place where the landslide had almost caught him, then crossed a narrow ledge where thick bushes grew. After several hundred feet, the holds started down the cliff again.

For some reason the Indians had not wanted anyone to know about their secret way into the valley. When the path was low enough to be visible from the ground, it was far from the open space around the rushing stream and hidden by the thick pine forest.

Bob stepped from the cliff to the forest floor. He looked at his watch again. Now he really was late!

He sped back to the water bottle, picked it up, and raced along the animal trail through the forest. At last he left the trail to follow in reverse the landmarks he'd memorized.

When he glimpsed the meadow where the Cessna had crash-landed, it was about an hour to sundown. He was exhausted, but excited. Wait till he told the other guys what he'd survived!

◆ ◆ ◆

When Bob and Pete separated, Pete had followed the animal path he'd discovered while gathering wood. It led, as Pete had suspected, southeast into the dense pine forest.

Sunshine filtered through the tall branches, casting warm light and cool dark shadows. Overhead, the treetops touched, occasionally blocking the sky. The air was aromatic with the rich smells of pine and earth.

Pete continued on the dirt path for a half hour, watching for human tracks. He saw deer, raccoon, and cougar prints, also deer and bear scat. But disappointingly, no prints from hiking boots or tennis shoes. He'd hoped for the smell of campfire smoke, the sound of a Jeep revving up, the sight of a telephone pole. But there was nothing.

Except, suddenly, the sense that someone was moving toward him from behind, parallel to the path and at great speed. Someone or some animal.

He heard rustlings.

He stopped on the trail and listened, all his senses razor alert. He stepped quietly off the path. He stood behind a tree, watching.

The rustlings came closer—almost opposite him. And they passed by.

Just like that, the faint sounds moved beyond Pete, speeding on into the forest. Pete saw nothing.

The hairs on the back of his neck stood on end. Who—or what!—was out there?

"Hey!" Pete yelled. He figured that if it was an animal, the shout would make it panic and run. "Stop!" A person would stop to find out who was shouting, and why.

Pete listened. Nothing bolted. Nothing tore panic-stricken through the trees. But the rustling sounds continued to move steadily away as if he'd never called out.

Pete ran after the sounds. His legs stretched and ate up the trail. He had an athlete's body, with an athlete's need for activity. It felt great to be moving.

He slowed and listened. There they were—the same faint sounds.

He raced off the path and plunged into the forest. Pine needles brushed his face.

And then he saw it—a figure. A person. It was a male, almost invisible as he moved steadily through the dark shadows of trees.

"Stop!" Pete bellowed, running after the ghostly figure. "I want to talk to you! We need help!"

The figure seemed to hesitate, lose a beat in his slow, paced running. And then he speeded up. He disappeared into the darkest tree shadows.

Pete tore after him. What kind of person wouldn't

answer when he was asked for help? Swiftly Pete rounded the stand of trees.

The ghostly figure was gone. Vanished. This guy—or ghost!—was a real creep.

Pete stood still to watch and listen. Nothing. Either the guy had suddenly levitated or he was hiding.

"All I want to do is talk!" Pete called. "My friends and I are lost!" He waited.

Nothing.

"We won't hurt you . . ."

Silence. I'll find him, Pete thought.

He began exploring the nearby shadows and trees.

Suddenly he remembered the time. He looked at his watch. It was late. He needed to get back.

But *where was back*?

What an idiot, he told himself angrily. He wasn't even sure where the *path* was! Like a fool, he'd forgotten to watch for landmarks.

Pete had a terrible sinking feeling in his stomach as he realized what he'd done.

He was lost!

5

Missing Persons

PETE BREATHED SLOWLY. HEY, CALM DOWN, HE told himself. You got here. Now figure out how to get back!

He looked again at his watch. He moved to a spot where the treetops opened enough to give a clear view of the sun's position.

He calculated. He'd been headed southeast when he followed the trail from the meadow. The sun had been on his right shoulder. The sun was lower now. For him to head northwest, it would be low on his *left* side, almost on his chest.

Locating the meadow again in this vast, timbered terrain might be impossible, but he had to try.

Pete moved carefully, checking the sun's position. Birds sang, and the wind ruffled the trees. Small animals scooted away from his footsteps.

He walked for an hour. I don't recognize a thing, he told himself with dismay. Not a single landmark!

The sun was even lower, perhaps an hour to sundown, when he again heard sounds of movement in the forest. He started to call out, then decided not to. The last time I tried that, he thought, the guy got away.

Quietly he padded after the sounds.

They were leading him north, and they were far noisier than those of the first ghost he'd heard.

He must be crazy! He should be getting back to the meadow, not getting himself even more lost!

The sounds stopped.

Pete hesitated only a moment. He barreled through the forest toward them.

And skidded to a stop, shocked.

"Bob!" Pete cried, astounded.

Bob looked back. "How's it going, Pete?" He smiled.

Pete laughed. It was great to find someone who answered you! He lowered his shoulders and turned on the speed.

"Whoa!" Bob shouted, laughing.

Pete slammed into Bob's midsection and carried him into the grassy meadow.

"Hey, I just ran into somebody I know!" Pete said. "You!" He roared with laughter.

Bob pushed him off. He shook his head, grinning. "You're nuts. Anyone ever tell you that?"

"You, just now," Pete said.

Pete threw a sweaty arm over Bob's shoulder. They walked toward the Cessna and exchanged reports.

"A landslide!" Pete said. "You could've been totaled!"

"And what about you?" Bob retorted. "A forest ghost gets you lost!"

They shook their heads at their bad luck.

"Look, Jupe's done better than us," Bob said, pointing ahead. "That smoke's dark enough to get the attention of any fire lookout!"

Jupiter was sitting next to a smoky fire. The afternoon was growing cold, and he now wore his jacket zipped to the chin. He'd carried their duffels from the plane and set up a makeshift camp. The ground was scraped free of duff—decaying leaves, grass, and other flammable materials—within a six-foot radius of the fire. Fresh pine boughs, piled nearby, waited to be arranged into beds.

"That was some tackle," Jupe observed as Bob and Pete approached.

"Pete was just glad to see me," Bob explained.

Jupe narrowed his eyes at Pete's muscular frame. "Well, I hope he's not that glad to see *me*!"

"Would you rather I *kiss* you?" Pete said.

"You do, and your lips'll shrivel up and fall off!" Jupe promised.

The three guys laughed loudly. Bob and Pete put on their jackets and stood close to the fire, warming their hands and telling Jupe about their adventures. It was really getting cold now.

Bob was looking around. "Where's Dad?"

"Still gone," Jupe said.

"He should've been back long ago," Bob said worriedly. He stared up at the cliff and thought about the ugly wound and bruise on his dad's head. He started to run.

"Hey, wait for me!" Pete said, following.

Jupe sighed. Someone had to stay and watch the fire. Untended campfires could start forest fires. This time he would've liked to have gone with Pete and Bob. He was worried about Mr. Andrews too.

Pete looked at the western sky. Only about a half-hour remained until sunset. Daylight would last a little after that, and then darkness.

Bob scrambled up the cliff. The rock was solid, not exposed to the same intense erosion as the cliff around the waterfall. Also, the granite rose in mounded, easy-to-climb layers. They were so smooth that they were sometimes slippery, the result of polishing by glaciers thousands of years ago.

At the top, Pete and Bob stood on the edge. They breathed heavily.

Bob looked anxiously around. "I don't see him," he said.

"Maybe he's sitting on a rock somewhere. Resting," Pete replied.

Below them was the view Mr. Andrews had climbed to see. Timbered mountains stretched for hundreds of miles in green accordion pleats. The low sun cast long shadows, turning valleys into black pits and peaks into golden embers. There was no sign of a fire tower.

They turned, surveying the cliff top. It was a long, mostly flat plateau of granite, with giant boulders and rocks scattered around. Occasional scrub trees forced their way from the rock, struggling to survive. One place on the plateau looked much like another. North of it, a half mile or so away, big pines grew thickly. It was another forest. It climbed uphill to a long ridge that stretched across the horizon. Somewhere on the far side of that ridge was Diamond Lake.

Bob and Pete split up.

"Dad!"

"Mr. Andrews!"

"Dad!"

A cold, stiff wind swept across the barren plateau. Bob shivered. Where was his dad? He wouldn't have left the area without telling someone first.

And then he saw it. His dad's blue Dodgers cap.

"Dad!" he hollered. He ran to the cap lying next to a skeletal manzanita bush. "Dad!" He had to be near. "Where *are* you?"

"Hey, what'd you find?" Pete asked, running up to him.

Bob showed him. "He loves this dumb cap. He wouldn't lose it. Something bad's happened. I know it. He's gotten sick. Or dizzy and confused. Or *lost*."

"Let me see," Pete said. He turned the Dodgers cap in his hands, examining it. "Looks okay." It wasn't torn, dirty, or bloody.

"Dad!" Bob called again.

"Hey, he could've just accidentally dropped it."

Bob shook his head stubbornly. "This is his lucky cap."

Pete picked up fist-size stones. "I'm going to build a pyramid so we can remember where you found it. You keep looking."

Bob nodded and moved off.

Pete glanced at the sun's bright orange glow. It was setting. Quickly he finished the pyramid, a universal marker for woodsmen and explorers. He continued searching. He didn't want Bob to know how worried he was.

Bob and Pete cupped their hands and called. The wind seemed to blow their shouts away. They looked behind enormous boulders, in the shadows of straggly trees, and down dark crevices where the granite plateau had separated during massive earth movements.

"We've got to go back!" Pete yelled at last.

"Not yet!" Bob protested. He moved closer to the forest that rimmed the plateau's north side, searching.

"Come on!" Pete bellowed. "Your dad would want us to go back!"

"No!" His father was nearby. Bob knew it!

"He'd be furious if we got lost too!" Pete shouted.

Bob stopped. His shoulders slumped.

"The sun's setting!" Pete insisted. "We won't be able to see anything!"

Bob turned, defeated by logic. But he wouldn't give up. Tomorrow I'll be back, he promised himself.

They trudged along the edge of the cliff until they found the place where they had climbed up. They descended, the last rays of light streaking across the indigo sky. The rising moon was almost full, but it didn't cast enough light to continue the search.

They hurried over the grassy meadow, shivering, to the camp Jupe had built. It was dark now. The fire-light made a warm circle.

"No luck?" Jupe asked.

"Just his cap," Pete said.

Pete told Jupe what they'd seen. Bob sat down on a rock and stared dejectedly into the fire.

Jupe raised his eyebrows at Pete. Pete nodded. They needed to cheer up Bob.

"Hey," Pete said suddenly, "I hear the Hot Pistons are really dynamite." He was referring to a rock group managed by the talent agency Bob worked for.

"Oh, they're all right, I guess," Bob said, distracted.

"Yeah," continued Jupe, "what's their new single?"

" 'Low to the Ground,' " Pete answered. "How does it go, Bob?"

"Look, guys . . ."

"C'mon Bob, it's dark and the rustlings are making me nervous," Pete lied.

"Well . . . 'Cruisin' in my Chevy down the Coast Highway . . .' " Bob began.

The other two Investigators chimed in and pretty soon raucous verses about low-slung hot rods and burning rubber filled the night air. Pete picked up a branch and started playing it like an electric guitar. Much to the amazement and delight of his friends, Jupiter tried to dance to the music for a while, gyrating his well-padded hips. Then, bright red in the face, he switched to drumming on a log instead. Bob was swept up in the hilarity of his pals' antics and for a time forgot the gloomy thoughts about his father.

After a few more hit songs, the guys started to get ready for bed.

"Take off the shirt you're wearing," Pete told them, "and put on all your other shirts. You don't want that moisture next to your skin."

Jupe grumbled about the cold but knew Pete was right—the temperature would drop even more during the night and the fire might go out.

As soon as the guys had zipped their jackets on over their dry shirts, Pete ordered, "Now do the same with your socks. Don't put back on what you wore today. Wet socks will wick off your body heat."

Making faces at each other's aromatic feet, Bob and Jupe did as Pete said. Then they tucked their shirts inside their jeans and their jeans inside their socks to keep out drafts.

Jupe got the night's popcorn and candy bars from the plane and handed them around. The guys ate. They then arranged the pine boughs into thick, springy mattresses.

Pete put the empty popcorn sacks back in the plane. "If you leave trash around," he said, "you get visitors. Wild animals can smell food on plastic or paper. They'll come looking for a feast. Next thing you know, they think *you're* the feast."

The guys wrapped themselves in their Mylar space blankets and lay down around the fire. The high orange and blue flames licked the black, starry sky.

They closed their eyes. They needed to be rested and alert tomorrow. They were going to find Mr. Andrews—first thing!

A thought struck Jupiter out of nowhere. "Hey, Bob," he mumbled drowsily. "What about your contact lenses?"

"No sweat, Jupe," Bob replied. "They're extended wear lenses. I don't have to take them out for another week."

"And we'll be outta this meadow before those lenses are outta your eyeballs," Pete said.

With a laugh, the Three Investigators settled down for the night.

Pete and Jupe both drifted into an uneasy sleep, but not Bob. He opened his eyes and looked at the Big Dipper, Ursa Major. "Wherever you are, Dad," he whispered softly, "don't worry. We're going to find you!"

Bob closed his eyes. An owl hooted. Coyotes howled. An animal moved through the trees. He thought he heard the faint rumble of a truck on a distant mountain road. At night sounds traveled farther, and people imagined things. . . .

He breathed deeply. He wasn't helping his dad or himself by lying rigidly awake. Slowly he relaxed. At last weariness took hold and he fell into a heavy, restless sleep, thinking, where *is* he?

6

The Ghost Runner

THE SUN ROSE PALE AND COOL OVER THE EASTERN slopes. The guys got up immediately, stamping their feet and rubbing their hands. The fire was just coals. None of them had fed it during the night. Their space blankets and layers of clothing had kept them warm.

"We didn't have a freeze," Bob said. "That's good for Dad."

They ate the last of the cooked popcorn for breakfast. They'd save the candy bars for that night. They spread their space blankets over bushes to dry in the sun and took off their extra socks and shirts.

Bob emerged from the Cessna with a small spiral-bound notebook. "Dad's," he explained. "It's got yesterday's date on the first page, and a man's name—Mark MacKeir. Know him?"

"No," Jupe and Pete answered together.

"Maybe he was the guy Dad was going to meet," Bob said. "It's the right date, and it's the only notebook Dad brought." He put it into his jacket pocket, and the three of them headed up the meadow to the cliff.

Bob climbed the granite first and stood waiting for the others next to the pyramid marker. His hands rested on his hips and he held his chin up as he surveyed the barren, rock-strewn area. Wearing his father's blue cap, he looked like a younger, slimmer version of his dad.

"Okay," he said decisively, "we're going to spread out from the marker again. Pete and I covered this area last night." His arm swept in an arc. "I'm going to head farther north, toward the trees. You guys go left and right. We'll meet back here in an hour, okay?"

The three friends checked their watches and then separated to search among the rocks and huge boulders. They called Mr. Andrews' name and plodded over the hard surface, unwilling to pass even a crevice without checking.

They covered a lot of territory. When each returned, he had high hopes that even though his luck had been bad, one of the others had found Mr. Andrews. Or Mr. Andrews had found them.

But their luck wasn't bad—it was terrible.

The rock pyramid that marked where Bob had found Mr. Andrews' Dodgers cap was gone.

"Where is it?" Pete said with wonderment.

They walked slowly over the gray granite.

"It was here," Bob said.

"No, there," Pete said.

"You're both wrong," Jupe said. "It was right here.

I remember this circular moss stain on the granite. I *know* this is where we started searching."

He bent down, picked up a cigarette butt, and held it up. "Look. See how white the paper is? This couldn't have been here long. And it sure wasn't here when we started this morning. I would've seen it, and so would you."

"What're you saying?" Pete said, his eyes narrowed.

"He's saying we've had a visitor," Bob said thoughtfully. "Someone who smokes. Someone who destroyed our marker. Someone who sneaked around us or maybe just missed us. We were pretty spread out. And it would've been easy to stay out of sight behind all these big boulders."

"Just vandalism probably." Jupe examined the cigarette. A thin emerald band encircled the white paper next to the long filter. "Looks expensive." He dropped it into one of his voluminous shirt pockets.

"We'd better get moving," Bob decided. "Dad's not here. I vote we explore where Pete was yesterday. He saw somebody. Maybe it was Dad."

"Doubt it," Pete said.

"It *could*'ve been," Bob said reasonably. "You didn't get a good look. If Dad hit his head again, he could've gotten so confused that he wandered down there."

"But if it was your dad, why didn't he answer me when I yelled?" Pete said.

Nobody had an answer for that one.

"At least we can find whoever *was* there. And maybe

get hold of the forest service," Bob urged. "They can cover a lot more territory than we can."

Jupe and Pete looked at each other and nodded. It made sense. The forest service had the equipment and manpower to make a really thorough search.

◆ ◆ ◆

They stopped back in camp. The coals looked dead, but Jupe threw dirt on them just in case. Pete and Bob rolled stones into a big SOS in the middle of the meadow. They filled their pockets with popcorn kernels and candy bars. Bob got the water bottle.

"Space blankets too," Pete told them. "And the rest of the stuff in the emergency kit. I got turned around once down there. Let's go prepared for the worst."

Bob and Jupe nodded. Bob wished his dad had had a blanket the night before.

Sunshine filtered through the tall treetops, sprinkling bright globes of light among the cool forest shadows. Bob, Jupe, and Pete hiked single file over the narrow trail that Pete had covered alone the day before. Bob, still wearing the Dodgers cap, watched everywhere for his dad.

They were entering a clearing when they heard a plane flying overhead.

"Oh, no!" Jupiter said.

They ran to the center of the clearing and waved their arms at the plane streaking high in the sky.

They shouted. Pete whipped his silvery space blanket out of his jacket pocket and swung it frantically.

Bob and Jupe did the same. In his frustration, Bob leaped up and down. He needed help to find his father!

"We're down here!"

"Look down here!"

But the plane continued on, growing smaller and smaller.

"Maybe they saw our SOS!" Bob said, his voice full of hope.

But they all knew the plane was so high it probably hadn't.

Bob walked off down the path. "We'll just have to find Dad ourselves."

Determined, the three friends resumed hiking.

Pete's stomach rumbled. So did Jupe's.

"Hunger in stereo," Pete quipped.

Bob smiled. "You guys are weird."

Pete suddenly stopped, pressing a finger to his lips. He looked left through the pine boughs.

Bob followed Pete's glance. Distant branches moved in the shadows. *Dad!* There was a faint rustling. At last he saw the cause—a slender, wiry figure in a vest and pants moving swiftly from shadow to shadow. Bob was deeply disappointed. It wasn't his father.

Pete pointed to the trail so Jupe and Bob would know he wanted them to stay on it. And then he was gone, melting among the trees.

Jupe and Bob sped off along the path, trying to keep

pace with Pete. They heard off-trail rustlings and sighted Pete occasionally, but never again saw the figure he chased.

Pete slipped in and out among the trees, following the perpetual motion of the person. It was the same guy, Pete was sure. Pete ran soft-footed, better at it today than yesterday. The hunter and the quarry raced on until Pete saw the guy's rhythm break. He'd spotted Pete.

The guy took a sharp right, tearing around a large clump of trees, trying to lose Pete just as he had yesterday.

But this time Pete bore left, circling the clump on the opposite side. When he'd almost rounded it, he stopped abruptly. Slowly he turned. His eyes almost popped out of his head.

Pete was staring directly into the shining black eyes of a young man about his own age.

He was an Indian in a dark leather vest and jeans.

The guy stood stock still in the blackest part of the tree's shadow. He was so silent and immobile that he might have been a tree himself. Not a muscle in his face moved, not even his eyes.

Pete breathed hard. "Hey, we need some help . . ." he began.

The Indian's mouth remained closed. Fast as the wind, he rotated on one heel, burst from his frozen position, and dashed almost soundlessly away over the forest duff.

Pete chased after him, but the trees seemed to swallow the guy. The Indian was the fastest runner Pete had ever seen.

Pete raced on, more and more convinced the chase was hopeless, more and more angry that the Indian had refused to talk, to help.

Meanwhile, Bob and Jupe continued along the trail, moving briskly. Bob set the pace, and Jupe panted behind. It seemed an endless trek, especially during the long periods when Pete was out of sight.

And then Pete suddenly appeared on the trail a hundred feet ahead of them, breathing hard. His red-brown hair was tousled and his strong face glistened with sweat.

"Did you see him?" Pete asked as Bob and Jupe ran up.

"Who?"

"The Indian guy!"

"What?" Bob said, astounded.

"It looks like I've lost him for sure," Pete said. "Let's keep moving."

The little group pressed on along the forest path, following the rise and fall of the gently rolling mountain slope. Pete told them what had happened.

"So he kept heading in this direction," Bob said thoughtfully.

"Makes you kind of wonder what's ahead," Pete added.

"All I can say," Jupe said miserably, "is that I hope whatever it is, it's not far!"

They rested five minutes for Jupe's benefit and then resumed their dogged hike.

The sun rose past its midmorning position, slowly heating the forest. Butterflies floated by. Blue jays screeched. The dense smells of pine and sweat mingled in the new warmth.

Impatient and restless, Pete strode ahead and then waited for Bob and Jupe to catch up. After the third time he shouted for them to hurry.

"What is it?" Bob said when he sighted Pete.

"It better be good," Jupe added grumpily.

"It is!" Pete hollered. "How does a road strike you?"

Bob and Jupe hurried to Pete, who stood on the edge of a narrow, rutted dirt road. It came out of the trees from the northeast and vanished back into the forest to the southwest. It wasn't much, but it was marked with fresh tire tracks.

"I don't remember seeing a road here from the air," Bob said.

"By the time we got in the vicinity," Jupe reminded him, "we weren't doing much sightseeing. We were getting ready to crash!"

They looked up and down the road, which was overhung by bushes and trees and was about the width of a car and a half.

"Downhill." Jupe was following what his tired legs were telling him.

"Okay by me," Pete said.

"Let's move," Bob urged. Somewhere nearby was help to find his dad. He had to get to that help.

They went downhill. Soon the road angled more sharply west.

The dirt was dry and hard-packed. They guessed the deep ruts had been formed during autumn and spring rains. In the winter the ground would be frozen solid and under several feet of snow.

The guys walked side by side, spaced out across the top of the ruts where the earth was fairly smooth. They were tired and hungry. They talked little, concentrating on their hiking. Birds flew through the treetops. The sun climbed higher.

The noise started almost as a little echo. They looked at one another, wondering what it was. As they continued down the road, it became recognizable—the sounds of people, dogs, children.

The noise wasn't loud enough for a city or even a town, but it meant people—at last!

The three guys hurried. Bob started to smile.

The road swung around a wide bend. At the end was a cluster of ramshackle wood huts, old trailers, and prefab cabins scattered amid a grove of towering redwood trees. Outside the houses stood fishing tackle, hunting gear, pens of chickens, frames with hides stretched for drying, and very old, battered pickup trucks and Jeeps that looked as if they should have been retired years ago.

It was a small Indian village. Two children dressed in shorts and T-shirts looked up from their play to gape at Bob, Jupe, and Pete. They had red eyes and runny noses. The brown dog next to them jumped up to sniff the three guys' athletic shoes.

The village was humming with activity. Women and children started gathering in a central area. A drum began to beat.

"You!" Pete suddenly yelled. "Stop!"

Pete took off, running behind one of the cabins. He grabbed the shoulder of a young Indian who wore a leather vest and jeans. He spun the fellow around roughly, jerking him off balance. The guy glared at Pete with a ferocious expression on his face.

"You!" Pete glared back. "You're the one we've been chasing!"

7

Sick People

"WHAT KIND OF GUY ARE YOU!" PETE DEMANDED of the Indian youth. "Running off like that!"

The Indian did a double take. With his straight black hair, piercing black eyes, and slightly curling lip, he looked ferocious. But then he recognized Pete. His eyes widened in astonishment. Then his expression softened and his white teeth flashed in a smile.

"How'd you get here?" he asked Pete. "Did you track me? No. No, of course not. Hey, you found us! I would've gone back for you, soon as I could. Sorry I had to leave you behind."

It was Pete's turn to look amazed. "What do you mean, you had to?" Pete asked.

"Let me explain," the young man went on pleasantly. He straightened the short leather vest that he wore over his old, faded jeans. His belt buckle was unusual and beautiful—a large silver oval with a turquoise stone in the center. He touched the silver buckle and said, "I've been on a vision quest. . . ."

Just then Jupiter and Bob caught up with them.

"My name's Daniel Grayleaf," the young Indian said politely. "I—"

"Do you have a telephone?" Bob blurted out. "We have to reach the forest service. Our plane crashed, and now my dad's lost. We can't find him anywhere!"

Daniel shook his head. "Sorry. No telephones here, or even radios. We drive out when we need something."

"Then could you take us to the nearest ranger station?" Bob asked.

"No one leaves now," said a deep, raspy voice behind the three visitors. "Who are these strangers?"

The Investigators turned and saw a man of medium height, sturdy and muscular, with broad features. His eyes were red-rimmed and watery.

"Uncle, these are the ones I told you about," said Daniel.

"You didn't speak to them?"

"Not in the forest, no."

"Good." The man smiled at Daniel. But his face was grim when he looked at the "strangers."

Pete, Jupe, and Bob introduced themselves.

Daniel in turn introduced the village headman and chief hunter, Amos Turner.

"My father is missing," Bob said, his voice desperate now as he explained what had happened.

"What can we do to help them, Uncle?" Daniel asked.

Bob watched the headman eagerly.

"It is a problem," the older man said. "This has never happened in my time. I must consult."

The headman turned on his heel and left as abruptly and silently as he had arrived. Bob's face fell in disappointment.

"There's nothing we can do for now," Daniel Grayleaf reassured Bob. "With luck, Uncle will bring back good news."

Bob nodded worriedly.

"What's a vision quest?" Jupe asked to pass the time and distract Bob. Before Daniel could answer, Jupe's stomach rumbled. Somewhere something delicious was cooking. The dieting Investigator could smell it.

"I'll tell you about it," Daniel said, "but first can I get you something to eat?"

"You sure can!" Jupe said instantly.

"What about your popcorn, Jupe?" Pete kidded, and his stomach made a noise too.

Jupiter laughed. "You want to pop it? I can't wait that long!"

"Be right back," Daniel said, and hurried off toward the clearing where the drumbeat continued slowly.

"That guy can *move*," Pete said with awe.

Bob was obsessed with one thought. "They've *got* to give us a lift out of here!"

"They will," Jupiter said with more conviction than he felt. He looked around, wondering what the drumbeats meant.

Soon Daniel was back. "Come with me. The food's on the tables. First we dance, then feast, then make the ceremony. You're our special guests, so you get to feast now."

"You mean you have to wait till later?" Bob said, abashed. "That's not right."

"We'll wait," Pete insisted.

Jupe gulped. "Happy to wait," he echoed, trying to sound sincere.

Daniel laughed. "Don't be crazy. The food's ready. You're hungry. You honor us by feasting first."

The three friends looked at one another.

"We shouldn't insult our hosts," Jupe said.

"Right," Pete agreed.

"Thanks, Daniel," Bob said. He hoped wherever his father was, someone was feeding him, too.

They followed Daniel through the village. Adults and children stared at them curiously. Men were filtering into the central clearing where the women and children had gathered. The men were bare-chested and wore feather headdresses and necklaces of feathers and colored stones. The women wore necklaces and dresses with elaborate beadwork. Some of the men were stepping in time to the drumbeat and shaking what looked like two sticks tied together. The sticks sounded a little like rattles.

"Clap sticks," Daniel explained. "They're warming up. But come over here. Take plates and fill them. You can eat and watch and I'll try to explain what's going on."

Women removed basket covers from big platters of food. The three friends filled their plates with steaming meats, potatoes, beans, and bread. Jupe was so happy to see real food again, he took giant portions. The heck with his diet!

"Venison?" Pete asked Daniel, pointing to one of the platters.

"Yes, and that's rabbit, and that's squirrel. Over there is the fish. We catch it in the Truoc. In our language, *truoc* means 'the river.' "

They sat on benches beneath a mammoth redwood tree. Their table was a wide packing crate labeled in big block letters: ENGINE PARTS, NANCARROW TRUCKING COMPANY. Nearby, an old Chevrolet truck was raised on blocks, its engine spread in pieces on another ENGINE PARTS box. On the other side of them was the Truoc, which seemed more like a very large stream than a river. It flowed clear and deep alongside the village.

"Is this the same river that comes out of that big valley north of here?" Bob asked Daniel, remembering the hidden valley.

"You know the valley?" Daniel said, suddenly suspicious.

"Well, sort of," Bob said carefully. He took a bite of the venison. "I saw it from a distance."

"No one can go in there," Daniel said. "It's sacred. We call it the Valley of the Ancestors. It's part of our reservation and where we bury our people. Sometimes we have ceremonies there."

"I didn't go in," Bob assured him. He took another bite of venison. "Your people must have been here a long time."

"How do you know?"

"The handholds and footholds on the cliff. I was almost caught in a landslide, otherwise I wouldn't have noticed them. Looked like they were carved a long time ago."

"They come from the beginning, when the Creator made our people," Daniel said. "He also made the rock slides to keep out those without knowledge. And he made the willow tree from which we weave the baskets we use to raise our dead into the valley. The Creator made everything." He smiled. "I see. You were looking for your father. The Ancestors would understand."

"But they wouldn't understand sightseers."

"No tourists," Daniel agreed firmly. "Ever."

Jupiter had eaten half his food and was feeling better. "Something pretty important must be going on if you can't leave the village."

"The people have been sick," Daniel explained. "We have red eyes, some of us cough, our chests hurt. Some have fire-building devils in their stomachs. The elders decided to have a singing way ceremony to get rid of the terrible sickness. The village is closed until noon tomorrow. None of us can leave."

"Shouldn't you go to a real doctor?" Pete asked.

Jupiter kicked him under the table. Pete flinched.

"It's all right," Daniel told them. "You have your doctors, we have ours. Ours is a singing doctor, a shaman. He's taken care of us since before I was born. He's very wise. Sometimes he sends us to Bakersfield to the clinic there, but usually not. We're always healthy, or soon healthy again. Until a few months ago."

"Does your rule about staying here mean us too?" Bob said. "And in an emergency, can't someone take us out?"

"That's what Uncle is finding out from the singing doctor."

Suddenly the drums pounded loudly. The clap sticks rattled in unison. An enormous howl, eerie and almost inhuman, reverberated across the village. The four young men stood, looking at the clearing.

The dancers danced up and down in a large circle. Their moccasined feet moved lightly with the beat.

"They go up and down at different times, you see?" Daniel said. "That's because the world is like a boat. If everyone leans to one side at the same time, it rocks and then turns over. That's not good."

Soon a few dancers moved into the circle's center to solo. They jumped and leaped, moving sharply and strangely.

"When the world was reborn," Daniel explained, "the Creator appointed the woodpecker to report how things were going. So now we have men with pure hearts who jump inside the circle and jerk their heads back and forth like a woodpecker. They spread their arms, fly around, and sing the woodpecker song. This reminds the woodpecker spirit that someone is sick and he should report it to the Creator. If the Creator knows, he can make the doctor very strong so the sick person can get well."

The dancing continued. The Indian men sweated, changing places around and inside the circle. The women and children watched, often clapping and singing. The sickest people lay on mats, their heads propped up on blankets so they could see. It was a colorful ceremony, full of intensity.

And then it was over.

The drums stopped. The dancers and audience moved to the food tables, and the women removed the basket covers from the platters. Jupe noticed that the dancers all seemed to have red eyes, and now some of them coughed.

The headman, whom Daniel called Uncle, and an old man with a stern expression soon appeared. They were fiercely elegant in their ceremonial feathers as they weaved through the crowd. From the villagers' respectful manner, the Investigators guessed the old man was the village's shaman, their singing doctor. Although the two men paused occasionally to talk to the dancers, they were moving steadily toward Daniel and the three guys.

At last they stopped in front of them.

"We cannot help you," the headman, Amos Turner, announced. "You must walk out alone. That is our decision."

8

The Vision Quest

"THE RISK IS TOO BIG," THE SINGING DOCTOR SAID. "The ceremony must be kept pure. We have many, many sick people."

His old face was weather-beaten, wrinkled, and—it seemed to Bob, Jupiter, and Pete—genuinely sorry. But that didn't help Mr. Andrews much.

"It would be better if you stayed here," the headman, Amos Turner, insisted. "Tomorrow someone will drive you out."

"We have to go today," Bob said. "My father could be really hurt."

"It is a big country," the stern headman continued, "much bigger than you think. How will you find Diamond Lake?" His strong features were locked in disapproval.

"We'll follow the road," Pete said.

"Then you will walk forty miles," the headman said.

"Forty miles!" Pete gulped.

Jupe's arches almost collapsed—and then he had an idea.

"Perhaps we could rent one of your pickups," he suggested.

For the first time since they'd arrived in the village, Bob's handsome face brightened. It was just like Jupe to come up with a simple, logical solution that everyone else had missed.

"We have driver's licenses," Bob said quickly.

"And money," Pete added, pulling out his billfold. It held the savings he had planned to spend on his Diamond Lake vacation. "We'll pay."

"And we'll deliver the truck to wherever you want to pick it up," Jupe said. "We'll take very good care of it. Here, let me give you our card. People have trusted us to solve their problems. Now we're asking you to help us solve ours."

Jupiter handed a small white business card to each of the two men. They were the new cards he had designed for The Three Investigators.

The headman held the card stiffly in front of him. The singing doctor didn't even look at it, but passed it to Daniel. Daniel read it aloud for them.

The headman shook his head. "It is a bad idea."

The singing doctor frowned. "Perhaps, but I think it will do no harm." He looked appraisingly at the boys, his old, faded eyes shrewd. "These three will go in any case. Better that they take what we can give."

The headman narrowed his lips. He didn't like it, but the decision was the shaman's. "Very well. I will arrange it." He left, skirting the crowd at the food tables.

"Thank you," Bob said, and smiled gratefully.

The old man smiled too, and for a moment his eyes danced. "You young ones," he murmured. "In so much trouble all the time." Then he turned to Daniel. "So?"

"I did as you said."

"Tell them what you did," the singing doctor ordered. "They are interested."

Daniel turned to the three guys. "I've been on a vision quest. For twenty-four hours I fasted and ran through the forest. I stopped only to pray. At night I slept so the Creator could give me a message."

"What was your dream, Grandson?" the shaman asked.

"Grandson? Are you related to *everyone*, Daniel?" Pete blurted out.

Daniel and the singing doctor laughed.

"It's one of the ways we show respect," Daniel said. The singing doctor nodded.

"So the headman isn't your uncle?" Bob said.

"And I am not the shaman's grandson. But he is like a grandfather to all of us."

The three guys nodded.

"My dream was strange, Grandfather," Daniel said formally. "It began in a large green lake. I waded in, and a fish jumped into my hands. I thought I was very lucky—the fish would make a good meal. I gave thanks. Then many fish jumped into my hands, and there were so many I couldn't catch them all. They kept jumping at me, my back, my chest, my face. They were hitting me, harder and harder."

"You thought they would beat you to death?" the shaman asked.

Daniel nodded. "I threw all the fish back and left."

"You acted properly. What did you learn?"

"What we get without effort is often worthless and sometimes even bad," Daniel said promptly.

The singing doctor nodded, pleased. "And what message did the Creator give you?"

" 'In the right place, but without blessing.' "

"Ahhh." The singing doctor repeated the message to himself. He seemed to pale as he thought about it. "Does it answer your question?"

The Investigators looked inquiringly at Daniel.

"I don't understand it," Daniel said sadly. "I'll never find him."

"The Creator gave you the answer," the shaman corrected. "Use it."

Daniel dropped his eyes. "Yes, Grandfather."

"You must dress for the next ceremony."

"Yes, Grandfather." Daniel turned to Jupiter, Bob, and Pete. He flashed them a dazzling smile. "Good luck." And then he was gone, running like the wind.

"Good-bye, young warriors," the singing doctor told them. "Trust only yourselves."

He moved into the crowd, smiling and speaking with his ailing flock.

"Look at the headman," Pete said, nodding at a corrugated-metal hut about fifty yards away.

The muscular headman stood in front of the hut, talking with a slight Indian who kept rubbing his hands on the front of his jeans. The small man nodded constantly as if the headman was giving him a series of instructions. At last the headman returned to the food tables, and the smaller man disappeared into the hut. Many wooden crates of various sizes were stacked on one side of the building. Each of them bore the name NANCARROW TRUCKING COMPANY in big block letters.

Jupiter sat down to finish his meat and potatoes. He picked up his fork and leaned over to dig in. That's when he saw the cigarette butt. It was lying on the ground right next to the Nancarrow packing box.

He reached down and picked it up. It was yellow and battered, but it had the same emerald band and long filter as the butt he'd found early that morning.

"Hey, Jupe," Pete said. "What's up?"

"Look," Jupiter said simply. He held out his hand with both butts on the palm.

"Wow!" Pete said.

"What does *that* mean?" Bob wondered.

"Beats me," Jupe said, "but I think I'll hold on to them. You never know."

A young woman emerged from the crowd and walked toward Jupe, Pete, and Bob.

"I'm Mary Grayleaf, Daniel's sister," she said to all of them, but her gaze was on Bob. She smiled at the handsome Investigator. "Here." She dropped a key into his hand. "Our headman said to tell you the pickup will be ready for you soon. Have you had plenty to eat?"

"Plenty," Bob assured her, returning her gaze. Her face was strikingly pretty and was framed by long straight hair. She wore a necklace of turquoise stones over her loose white dress. Bob noticed that her eyes were red too, almost as red as the embroidery that decorated the hem and sleeves of her dress.

"Are you really Daniel's sister," Bob asked, "or is that another term of respect?"

For a moment Mary Grayleaf looked puzzled. Then she gave a light, merry laugh. "Really, I am."

Jupiter and Pete looked at each other. Jupiter raised an eyebrow. Pete stifled a chuckle. Bob had done it again, and without even trying. Wherever he went, he was a magnet for pretty young women.

"Is there going to be more ceremony now?" Bob asked her.

"The shaman is going to sing and dance," she said, still looking into his eyes. "Then he'll pray. He's preparing himself to receive a message from the Creator that will tell him what's making our people sick. When he knows, he'll put an enchantment on whoever or whatever it is, and then he can begin our cure."

"And enchantments work?" Bob said, smiling.

"Always," she said seriously. "And cures, too."

Jupiter couldn't stand it any longer. "What about vision quests?"

That got her attention. "You heard Daniel's quest message? What was it?"

Jupiter thought a moment, then repeated, "In the right place, but without blessing."

She considered the words, and then shook her head. "I don't know what it means. Did Daniel?"

"No. The singing doctor told him to think about it," Bob said. "Why's it important?"

"Because . . ." Mary frowned, closing her eyes. She opened them. "Our uncle, our *real* uncle, is missing. He helped our mother raise Daniel and me after our father moved off the reservation. Father disappeared years ago. Now our uncle has disappeared too. He's been gone over a month, and Daniel keeps searching the forest."

"Something weird's going on around here," Bob said. "My father's missing too."

She nodded, her dark eyes sad. Something in the crowd caught her attention. It was the slight man who had been taking instructions from the headman. The Investigators had not seen him leave his hut. Now he raised a hand to Mary, signaling.

"Your pickup is ready," she said, rubbing her reddened eyes.

She led them around the other side of the village, past tethered dogs and a tall mound of dirt that was the diameter of a large house. "That's the sweat lodge, where the men purify their bodies," she said.

"I have another question," Jupe said. His hand slipped into his voluminous shirt pocket and brought out the two cigarette butts. "Do you know who smokes these cigarettes?"

"No," Mary said, puzzled.

Disappointed, Jupe put them back into his pocket.

They passed a bright red new Ford pickup. It stood out among the old trucks and Jeeps in the village. "The headman's," Mary said. "He's a good man and the best rifle shot in the village. He buys us new clothes, tools, and parts for our trucks when they break down."

"Where does he get the money?" Jupe asked her.

She shrugged. "I don't know. Part-time jobs in Diamond Lake, I guess. It's none of my business." She patted the fender of a dented, rusted Ford F-100. "This is his old truck. He's lending it to you. Take good care of it. You're to leave it at the ranger station in Diamond Lake."

After stowing their gear in the back, the guys climbed into the cab. There were no seat belts. Pete sat behind the wheel. He was their mechanic and the best driver.

"Take our road north until it runs into a two-lane logging road," she told them. "Take that road west. It's dirt too, and will lead you to the highway. Turn right, and follow the highway into Diamond Lake."

They thanked her. Pete started the motor. Mary

smiled and waved good-bye, looking at Bob. The three drove off, the old truck backfiring. Dust spun up behind the wheels. Dogs barked.

"Wheels," Pete said with satisfaction. "At last."

"Yeah," Jupe said. "It's almost enough to make up for Bob's disgusting popularity."

"Sorry, guys," Bob said cheerfully. "What can I say? If you've got it, flaunt it."

Jupe and Pete turned and made faces at him. Bob sat back in the seat, thinking about Mary. Pete leaned forward to concentrate on the narrow road, steering high over the ruts. The road wound out of the redwoods and back into the pines, rising and falling with the gentle hills.

"I don't think the headman likes us," Pete said.

"But the shaman does," Jupe said. "He made sure we got the truck. Did you see his expression when Daniel told him his quest message? That guy knows what it means, and he isn't happy."

"You think something's happened to the uncle?"

"A month's a long time to be gone," Jupe said. "And what's making all those Indians sick? They could just have a virus, but I wonder. . . ." He lapsed into silence, pinching his lower lip. He always did that when he was thinking hard.

A couple of miles past their starting point, the road began to climb. They drove up the steep grade. The early afternoon sun shone brightly, warming the fragrant pines.

At the top of the hill, the truck backfired loudly.

They started down the steep decline. The truck quickly picked up speed.

Pete pressed the brakes. The old truck slowed. He released the brakes, and free again, the truck went faster and faster.

They whizzed past trees and bushes.

Pete hit the brakes. For a moment the truck slowed. Suddenly the brake pedal snapped free. Pete's foot slammed all the way to the floor. The truck raced downward again. The unconnected brake pedal lay uselessly on the pickup's floor.

"I don't believe it!" Pete gasped. "The brakes are gone!"

9

Rough Riders

THE PICKUP PLUNGED FASTER AND FASTER DOWN the steep hill, locked in the deep ruts.

Pete hung on to the wheel. Next to him, Jupe slammed from side to side like an unhappy beach ball. Bob, on Jupe's other side, grabbed the passenger door's armrest. The three guys bounced and smashed their heads on the ceiling.

"The emergency brake!" Jupe said.

"We're going too fast," Pete shot back. "It won't do a thing!"

"Then what?" Bob yelled.

"Maybe the road will level out!" Jupe said, his teeth rattling.

"First I gear down," Pete shouted. "If I can!"

Sweat broke out on Pete's forehead as he grabbed the stick, hesitated, then rammed it from third gear into second.

The motor screamed with the increased revolutions. truck lurched, then slowed.

But not enough. The pickup still hurtled down the hill.

"Look out! There's a bend!" Bob cried. The road ahead angled right and disappeared around a hill.

The three guys shouted, "Whooooa" as the pickup whipped around the long downward curve. Tree roots extended out of the hill above the road where erosion had washed away the soil.

Pete turned the steering wheel right, toward the hillside.

"I'm gonna run the side of the truck against the hill!" he said. "It'll slow us down!"

The pickup popped out of the ruts.

"Watch it!" Jupe shouted.

Dirt, rocks, and small boulders from the eroded bank lay piled along the edge of the road. The truck plowed into them.

Pete fought the wheel. It spun out of control. The truck bounced and shook like an old washing machine.

Again Pete wrenched the wheel toward the embankment. Too late, the truck went into a skid. It thudded back into the deep ruts.

"Here we go again!" Pete said grimly.

Locked in the ruts, the pickup flew around the next bend, passing the embankment.

"Look!" Bob said. "We're going to go *up*!"

Ahead lay a short hill that sloped gently upward.

"At last!" Jupe said, his round face glistening with sweat.

The truck roared to the bottom of the steep hill and on up the short one as if it were on a roller coaster. Motor screaming, the truck maintained its ferocious speed.

The knuckles of Pete's hands were white on the steering wheel. Bob held on to the sill of the open window with a death grip. In the middle, Jupe sat and sweated, one hand on the dashboard and the other on the ceiling, trying to brace himself.

The embankment was far behind them. Brush grew thickly along the sides of the road. The pickup began to slow as it climbed the hill.

The guys breathed easier. If there was a long level stretch on the top, the truck would roll to a stop. . . .

"Oh, no!" Jupe cried as the truck reached the crest.

Although the truck had slowed, it still took the top of the hill as if its tail were on fire. It sailed over. It landed with jaw-throbbing crashes, first on its back wheels and then on the front wheels.

And it went hurtling down the other side, skidding along the road. The trees were a blur.

"Hang on!" Pete bellowed as he twisted the steering wheel to match the car's skids.

Helpless without seat belts, the three were again tossed in every direction. The old vehicle shook as if it were having a seizure. It landed back in the ruts.

"It's going to fall apart!" Jupe said.

"Yow! It's going to fall *off*!" Bob cried, leaning out his window. The right side of the road had suddenly disappeared. Treetops barely peaked up over the top of the road. Pine, brush, and granite covered the steep, hundred-foot drop. Taking a trip down that mountainside would be fatal.

Pete kept to the ruts, grimly aware that now they were an asset—they kept the truck away from the precipice. The truck careened around a shallow curve and at last left the sheer drop behind.

"Look!" Pete said, excited.

And there it was—straight ahead, the end of their nightmare ride. Maybe.

A tall granite cliff loomed in front of them, running east-west. The road angled right, traveling alongside it. If Pete could just ease the truck against the rock . . .

"You've got to be kidding!" Jupe said. "You'll take the truck's side off!"

"A spark in the wrong place, and the gas tank'll explode!" Bob chimed in.

"You got a better idea?" Pete said, his jaw jutting in determination.

Jupe and Bob were silent. They stared at the granite that now climbed along the left edge of the road.

The Ford roared onward. Again Pete jumped it out of the ruts.

It banged into the granite cliff. It bounced off in a hail of sparks.

"Oh, boy," Bob muttered.

Pete concentrated on the cliff, a gray blur on his left. He turned the wheel slightly toward it, tryin steady the Ford. The truck touched the granite. Sparks flew once more. It touched again. Again.

The tension inside the truck was electric.

"Steady," Jupe said.

"You can do it, Pete," said Bob.

Pete turned the wheel one more time. The truck touched the cliff, and he held it there. The metal screamed in protest as it scraped the granite. Sparks cascaded.

The three guys sweated.

And the truck slowed. Like an exhausted rogue elephant, it relaxed into a noisy, smelly amble.

The tires crunched and the metallic body groaned against the granite as gravity pulled it on.

At last the Ford simply stopped, the motor idling. Pete turned it off. The pickup's front left fender rested against the cliff.

Pete, Jupe, and Bob sat in the cab, savoring the sudden silence. Dust swirled in the air. No one moved or said anything for a moment.

"Pete, you wrecked this vehicle," Jupe said solemnly.

"You'll have to pay for it," Bob added.

"Your insurance'll go up."

"Your good driver record is ruined."

Pete turned slowly and looked at them, incredu-
's.

nd how can we ever thank you?" Jupe said, slap-
e on the back.

"Talk about a ride!" Bob grinned, and punched him in the arm.

Pete started laughing. "You're welcome, you idiots. Are you gonna sit there all day? I want to see what she looks like. In case you haven't noticed, I can't exactly get my door open."

They piled out of the battered truck and walked around to the back.

Pete shook his head. "Jupe, wait till I tell your cousin Ty about this!"

From front fender to back, a broad band of the driver's side was rubbed clean of paint and rust, the steel polished to silver. Gashes streaked the flattened body. The door's edges had melted into the frame, and the door handle was long gone.

"Uh-huh," Pete said, and returned to the cab.

"Uh-huh?" Jupe repeated, following him.

Pete sprawled across the cab floor, his head and hands under the steering wheel where the foot pedals were. He picked up something from the floor.

"Well?" Jupe said impatiently.

Pete slid back out of the cab and stood up. He held up part of a bolt.

Jupe examined it. There were tiny saw marks where a blade had cut the bolt almost all the way through. He passed it to Bob.

"This has to do with our lack of brakes, I take it," Jupe said.

"You bet," Pete said. "The brake pedal is attached

to a shaft that leads to the master cylinder. When you step on the pedal, a piston in the cylinder forces brake fluid out and into the brake lines—"

"Get to the point, will you?" Bob said.

"All right, all right," Pete grumbled. "You need that bolt to attach the pedal to the shaft."

"And somebody cut it enough so that at the first big stress, it'd break," Jupe said quietly.

"That's it," Pete confirmed.

Bob groaned. It seemed like they were farther than ever from finding his dad.

The three friends looked at one another. They were in big trouble.

"It had to be one of the Indians," Jupe said.

"The headman?" Pete wondered. "He didn't like us. But enough to kill us?"

"It couldn't have been Daniel," Bob said, thinking.

"Or Mary," Jupe added.

"Not Mary," Bob repeated firmly.

"We can't go back there for help," Pete said.

"Not since one of them just tried to kill us," Jupe agreed. "It'd be better to go to Diamond Lake. Can you fix the brake pedal, Pete?"

"With a new bolt. But where do we get one?"

Pete and Bob searched the truck. They found nothing, not even a jack.

"Do you think the Cessna would have the bolt you need?" Jupe asked Pete. "I think there were some tools in the back." Jupe started strolling west along the cliff.

Pete and Bob glanced at each other and then stared after Jupe.

"It's the same cliff!" Pete said, excited.

"Looks like it," Jupe said. "We can follow the cliff back to the meadow, get the bolt, come back here, fix the truck, and drive to Diamond Lake for help to find Mr. Andrews." Jupe sighed, pleased with his plan but mentally exhausted by the amount of hiking it would take.

Bob got the water bottle out of the back of the truck. The guys tied their jackets around their waists and walked back uphill, following the road as it ran along the cliff. They saw the scars left by the pickup. When they passed the missing door handle, Bob kicked it into the brush on the other side of the road.

When the dusty road swung south toward the Indian village, the guys left it to follow the cliff west into the forest.

Soon the pines grew thick, their tall tops arching overhead. Birds sang, and the forest swayed with a light wind. It was a warm midafternon, but it was cool in the shade of the trees.

Suddenly a shot exploded.

A bullet whined past Pete's ear and thudded into a nearby pine. Bark chips flew into the air.

Jupe, Pete, and Bob hit the ground. A second bullet whizzed above them. They stared at one another.

Someone was shooting at them!

10

Trigger-happy

"WHERE ARE THEY?" SAID A ROUGH VOICE IN THE forest behind Jupiter, Bob, and Pete.

"Come on, Biff," a second voice answered. "Move it. We'll find 'em!"

The voices echoed through the trees. It was hard to pinpoint where they came from.

"Why would anyone shoot at us?" Bob whispered, his face flat on the ground.

"Don't know," Jupe whispered back, "but it'd be pretty unhealthy sticking around to find out."

The three looked at one another, nodded, and silently rose to their feet.

"Let's go!" Pete urged, taking off through the pines.

Bob and Jupe hustled after him. They ran parallel to the cliff face, heading for the meadow.

Again, gunshots rang out overhead. Pine needles showered down.

The guys ducked and dropped to their hands and

knees. They scuttled to safety around a house-size boulder.

"Where'd they go?" the rough voice grumbled loudly behind them from the dense forest.

"Rotten kids!" the other man complained.

The men were heavy-footed. Twigs snapped. Gravel spun and crunched. The men didn't care whether they were heard or not.

The guys took off again, Pete weaving a path for them through the pines.

"There they go!" the rough voice shouted. "Get 'em!"

Shots whined. Bullets bit into the earth around the guys. Dirt exploded into the air.

"Faster!" Pete ordered.

He raced through the shadows. Bob and Jupe followed. To keep their bearings, they stayed in sight of the cliff face. Jupe breathed hard but gamely kept up with his two friends. At last they paused behind a thicket of manzanita.

"Either of you see what they looked like?" Jupe panted.

"Negative," Bob reported. He took off his father's hat and wiped his wet face. "You okay, Jupe? Your face is as red as a tomato."

"No sweat," Jupe gasped. "Just like taking a stroll through the park."

"Let's keep moving," Pete said.

The three pushed off at a fast walk.

"Do you think we lost them?" Bob wondered.

"With luck," Jupe said.

"They didn't sound like they intended to give up," Pete said.

The Investigators continued west, paralleling the cliff. They stayed close to whatever cover they could find. They hiked a couple of miles. They passed wildflowers, thick pine groves, piles of boulders, and a sparkling creek where they refilled their water bottle.

"How much longer?" Pete asked.

"If we're right, it should be soon," Jupe said.

They moved again.

"There it is!" Pete cried.

They emerged at the southern edge of the big, familiar meadow.

"Where's the plane?" Jupe said instantly.

They stared ahead, shocked. The Cessna was missing. Even the broken-off wing was gone! How could that be?

"Wait," Pete cautioned, peering closer. "It's camouflaged!"

"Someone's piled brush over it!" Bob told them. "And look! Our big SOS is gone!"

"Now nobody can spot us," Pete said.

"You know," Jupe let out slowly, "I get the feeling somebody doesn't like us."

"Yeah. But who?" Bob wondered. "And why?"

"Are you fellows lost?" a deep bass voice asked.

The guys whirled around.

A big blond man with wraparound sunglasses was hiking toward them through the forest from the southeast.

"Anything I can do to help?" he said with a friendly smile. He was dressed in khaki, wore a backpack, and had a leather rifle case slung over his left shoulder. The flap on the case was loose and made a slapping sound as he walked.

"Where did you come from?" Pete asked, astonished.

"I've been hunting, but no luck today," the man said. "Never been here before. This part of the Sierras is new to me." He stuck out a big, meaty hand. "Name's Oliver Nancarrow, Ollie to my pals." With a friendly grin, he shook hands with the three guys. They introduced themselves to him.

Bob smiled eagerly. "Do you have a car here, Mr. Nancarrow . . . er, Ollie?"

"I parked up there," Nancarrow said, and nodded at the tall cliff. "A long ways off. There's a dirt logging road north. That's where I am. It goes into the highway to Diamond Lake."

"We don't mind hiking to your car, do we, guys?" Bob said. "Let's go."

"Wait a minute," Nancarrow said. "If I'm going to give you guys a ride, you might give me a clue why you need one."

Bob described their crash and the disappearance of his father. Finally he said, "We've got to move fast. Dad could need help bad."

"Has something else happened?" Nancarrow persisted. "I heard gunshots an hour or so ago."

The three guys looked at one another. If they told Nancarrow about the men chasing and shooting at them, Nancarrow might not want to have anything to do with them.

"Just hunters probably," Jupe said.

"We need to hurry," Bob urged.

Nancarrow hesitated only a moment. "Okay. Seems to me there's more going on than you're telling me. But I don't mind you keeping it to yourselves. Of course I'll help."

Nancarrow led them across the meadow, heading toward the cliff—Bob on his right, Jupe on his left, and Pete trailing behind.

"Your name is sure familiar," Jupe said as they walked. "Are you famous?"

"Hardly." Nancarrow chuckled. "I own a couple of little restaurants in Bakersfield. What did you say you and your father came up here for, Bob?"

Bob told him that his dad was a newspaper reporter and that he'd arranged to meet a news source in Diamond Lake.

As they walked and Bob talked, Nancarrow took out a cigarette. Pete's eyebrows shot up—it was very dangerous to smoke in such dry country. But Jupe looked back and signaled Pete to say nothing. The cigarette Nancarrow was lighting had a long filter and an emerald band encircling the white paper next to it—just like the cigarette butts Jupe had found on the granite plateau where Mr. Andrews' blue Dodgers cap had been and, later, on the ground in the Indian village. Jupe knew he'd heard—or seen—the name Nancarrow somewhere. Was it in the Indian village?

"We think Dad was meeting a guy named Mark MacKeir," Bob finished. He took his father's small notebook from his pocket and checked it. "Mark MacKeir, that's it. Does the name mean anything to you?"

"How strange," Nancarrow said. "Actually, it's awful. I don't know him, but I heard on the radio this morning that a Mark MacKeir was killed yesterday as he was driving up to Diamond Lake. I believe they said he was taking a vacation. He lost control of his car and it pitched over the side of the road and exploded. He died instantly."

"Oh, no," Bob breathed.

They were silent, thinking about Mark MacKeir's fiery death. Jupiter's gaze was caught by the unfastened flap on Nancarrow's rifle case. It was flopping up and down as Nancarrow walked. Each time the flap lifted, it showed part of the dark metal inside. Jupe had just finished reading a book on arms and armaments. The rifle was an unusual shape—it had an enormous bulge in the center, which meant the leather case had probably been custom built to accommodate its strange dimensions.

"Right now you and Mr. Andrews are more important," Nancarrow said. "Who knows you guys are here?"

"A few people," Jupiter answered before Bob could say no one. "The newspaper, of course."

"That right, Bob?" Nancarrow said, turning to him.

While Nancarrow's head was turned, Jupe tried to lift the case's flap. He wanted to look inside.

Something was nagging him about Nancarrow. Something more than the coincidence of the cigarettes. The packing crate they'd eaten lunch on at the Indian village had had NANCARROW TRUCKING COMPANY printed on the side. The same label had been on all of the wooden crates stacked outside one of the huts. That hut had belonged to the Indian who had signaled Mary that the headman's truck was ready. Nancarrow had lied. He had been here before—and often, by the look of things.

Bob glanced over at Jupe. Surprise showed in his eyes when he realized Jupe was trying to see inside the rifle case. He blinked and recovered fast. He knew what Jupe needed. He flashed his magnetic smile at Oliver Nancarrow.

"Sure," Bob said to him. "Dad told the city editor we were coming, and of course the managing editor because she has to okay the extra hotel bills."

Jupe was leaning over to see inside the rifle case when Nancarrow suddenly stopped walking.

Jupe dropped his hand from the flap and took an immediate interest in tying his shoelaces.

Nancarrow inhaled his cigarette one last time and ground it out beneath his heel. Pete couldn't stand the ecological insult. He picked up the butt when Nancarrow wasn't looking and dropped it into his pocket.

"When do they expect you back?" Nancarrow asked Bob as they hiked on. They were very near the tall, gray cliff.

"Well, we were supposed to call in yesterday," Bob said. He'd figured out that Jupiter didn't trust Nancarrow, and he'd learned long ago that Jupiter was more often right than wrong. So now he told Nancarrow a convenient lie.

While Nancarrow was occupied with Bob, Jupiter —with the skill of a pickpocket—lifted the long top flap of the rifle case.

"Then they'll be sending someone out to look for you?" Nancarrow asked Bob.

Jupiter carefully leaned over to look inside the leather case.

"There'll be search parties all over the mountains any time now," Bob said.

"We thought we'd speed things up a bit by going for help," Pete said, coming up to Nancarrow on the side opposite the rifle case.

Beneath the flap, Jupiter saw the carrying handle on top of the rifle. He could distinguish little else, but in a flash the strange shape made sense to him.

Suddenly Nancarrow stopped.

"Hold it!" he bellowed angrily. "What d'you think you're doing?" In one smooth movement he grabbed Jupiter's hand and flung it aside. He stepped back quickly to face all three guys. His eyes narrowed, and he whipped out a big, sleek rifle and pointed it at them.

"That's an M-16, all right," Jupiter muttered. The bulge in the leather case had been built to accommodate the M-16's distinctive handle, pistol grip, and fat magazine.

"What's going on?" Bob said.

"M-16s were introduced in the Vietnam War," Jupe continued, his heart pounding. "Now they're one of the most popular rifles in the world. But they're used for hunting people, not game. Who are you, Mr. Nancarrow? What do you want with us?"

"Okay, hotshots," he said, waving the rifle at them. "I tried to do this nice, now we'll do it the hard way. Get your tails up that cliff! You're coming with me!"

11

Fake-out

"COME ON, GUYS," JUPITER SAID MEEKLY. "WE don't want to make Mr. Nancarrow mad." He shuffled toward the cliff.

Bob and Pete stared at Jupiter, surprised by his sudden new personality. Once Jupe had been a child actor, playing the part of Baby Fatso in a movie series called *The Wee Rogues*. He didn't like to be reminded of the role, but he'd never forgotten how to act. He was a natural. Bob and Pete suddenly realized Jupe was acting now.

"Walk!" the big blond man ordered in a cold voice.

Pete and Bob walked. Nancarrow followed, aiming his gun at their backs.

"Is Mr. Andrews where you're taking us?" Jupiter said in a wimpy voice from in front.

"Forget it, kid," Nancarrow snapped, and gave a nasty, knowing laugh. "That's for me to know and for you to shut up about."

"So you did kidnap my dad!" Bob said, astounded. "What for?"

"Because he's as nosy as your friend!" Nancarrow snarled. "And he talks almost as much without saying a darn thing. Now shut up!"

They hiked west along the cliff, looking for a good place to climb. Jupe was panting noisily.

"Don't make us go so fast!" he complained.

"Cut the whining. We're not slowing down," Nancarrow said.

"Uh!" Jupe gasped. He let his heel slip over a moss-covered rock. He pitched backward, falling deliberately into Bob.

Bob staggered back. He missed Pete on purpose.

Pete's eyes blinked, then narrowed as he understood what Jupe and Bob had done.

Nancarrow frowned, not quite sure what was happening.

It was enough of a hesitation for Pete. He spun around. With the rapid-fire, polished motions that came from many hours in karate classes, he closed in on Nancarrow. Using his elbow's spring power, he slammed a backhand block, a *haishu-uke*, against the M-16, shoving the big rifle aside.

"Run for it!" he yelled at Bob and Jupe.

The two guys scrambled to their feet and tore across the meadow toward the western forest.

At the same time, Pete moved quickly into a front stance and delivered a hard lunge punch, an *oi-zuki*, into Nancarrow's thick chest.

Nancarrow staggered back, off balance, still firmly gripping the M-16.

Pete raced for the pines.

Bullets sprayed the trees. Needles, dust, and bark filled the air. Birds screeched and flapped away. The boys fell flat, safely hidden in some bushes.

"Biff! George!" Nancarrow called. "Where are you, you lazy bums? Get over here. Those kids made a break for it!"

Pete looked up. He could see the gunman in the meadow. "Nancarrow's got a walkie-talkie. He's calling out on it."

"Biff was one of the guys who was chasing us," Bob whispered. "He had the rough voice."

"And George must be the other one," Jupe said just as softly. "Makes you think maybe they were herding us toward Nancarrow. They sure seemed to lose us easily, almost like they let us go." Jupe told them what he had figured out about Nancarrow's cigarettes and the packing boxes in the Indian village.

"But Nancarrow couldn't have sabotaged the pickup," Bob decided. "He would've been too far away."

"I think it was that headman," Pete said.

"We'll have to figure that out later," Jupiter told them. "Let's get moving."

"What about Dad?" Bob asked.

"We know from the way Nancarrow was talking that he's alive," Jupe said. "First we get out of this mess, then we find him."

They looked out to the meadow, where Nancarrow still stood, staring into the trees.

"He's saving ammo," Jupe decided. "He won't shoot until he sees us."

The guys crept quietly to their feet and moved away through the pines.

"There they are!" the rough voice of Biff bellowed.

The guys ran a half-dozen steps. They froze.

Suddenly they were facing another M-16.

A dark-haired man with a deep tan and faded blue eyes rotated his rifle from one guy to another. Slowly he smiled, but there was no warmth in his face.

"I got 'em," the man said with satisfaction. By the sound of his voice, he was George.

Another man stepped out on their left, aiming his M-16 at them. "Right where we want 'em. Right, fellas?" It was Biff's voice. He was a skinny little runt of a man with short brown hair and wild eyebrows. "These kids don't have much in the way of brains."

From behind, through the forest, came the arrogant voice of Oliver Nancarrow. "Okay, move them back this way. We got a long hike ahead."

"You heard the boss," Biff said. "Move!"

Jupe, Bob, and Pete glanced at one another. Pete shrugged. There was nothing they could do.

"Move, I said!" Biff growled.

Then he made a mistake. The little guy jabbed the muzzle of his M-16 into Pete's back.

Pete whirled. He grabbed the barrel from the side. He slammed it back into Biff's belly, knocking the wind out of him.

Biff fell in a heap, his fingers wrapped convulsively around the M-16.

Instantly Bob kicked high, using a *yoko-geri-keage* side snap kick. He connected with George's tan chin. George staggered back. Bob followed and kicked again. George collapsed.

Jupe hid behind a thick pine. He thought about using his judo as Nancarrow strode toward the clearing. But at the last minute Jupe opted for an easier technique. He stuck out his foot. Nancarrow tripped.

As Nancarrow stumbled forward Pete slammed an elbow strike, an *otoshi hiji-ate*, down hard on the back of Nancarrow's neck. The big blond man pitched forward, his face in the dirt.

And the three guys sped into the forest.

Behind them Nancarrow swore loudly at his helpers. "Get them alive! We don't want to have to carry them!"

The Investigators ran south through the woods, dodging trees and rocks. Behind them they could hear the hard feet of their pursuers.

They kept moving, growing more tired and discouraged as the feet steadily pounded after them.

Pete turned west onto a dirt trail. Bob recognized it—it was the same one he'd used the day before when he'd filled the water bottle.

"We need a plan," Jupe panted. "We can't keep this up!"

"Got to rescue Dad, too!" Bob said.

There was an excited shout behind them. The guys poured on more speed.

"They found the path!" Pete said.

"They're going to grab us on this trail!" Bob warned.

"Let's forget the pickup," Jupe said, still running. "Pete, can you find that road Nancarrow was talking about?"

"The logging road that goes to the highway," Pete remembered. "Mary Grayleaf described it. The Indians' road was supposed to run right into it."

"That's it," Jupe said, breathing heavily. "You've got wilderness training. You're the strongest and fastest. You've got the best chance of making it to Diamond Lake."

"No prob," Pete said.

"And we'll get Nancarrow to chase *us*," Bob said. "Right, Jupe?"

"Right!"

The three guys gave one another quick high-fives and Pete was off. He left the path and melted into the trees. After Nancarrow and his thugs had passed by, chasing Jupe and Bob, Pete would return to the trail and head back up it for Diamond Lake.

Jupe and Bob ran on.

"We need a place to hole up," Jupe told Bob.

"How about a valley?" Bob said. "This is an emergency. I don't think the Ancestors would mind."

"Great!" Jupe said, puffing heavily.

Bob paused at a wide spot on the trail. "We'd better make sure Nancarrow follows us."

Jupe smiled. He caught his breath, then yelled, "Bob, I'm tired! I've got to rest!"

"You're always tired!" Bob yelled back. "I'm sick of you!"

Jupe's eyebrows shot up, slightly miffed even though he knew Bob was only pretending. "I don't care!" he bellowed. "Let's stop!"

They stood there, listening. The three gunmen were after them, all right. Their feet were thundering toward them like a herd of elephants.

"Oh, no!" Bob said. "Look!"

He held up his hand. He still had the water bottle.

"We should've given it to Pete!" Jupe said.

"Yeah, there's a stream where we're going. Who knows what Pete'll find?"

12

A Cliff-hanger

JUPE AND BOB'S SHOUTS AT EACH OTHER ECHOED through the trees to where Pete hid, listening.

Soon heavy feet rushed past his hiding place.

For a moment Pete pictured the deadly M-16s that Nancarrow and his gunmen carried. He hoped Jupe and Bob would be safe. Then he pushed the worry away. He had to concentrate on getting to Diamond Lake for help. It was up to him now.

He shook out his tight muscles and took off up the trail at an easy lope that ate up distance but didn't overtire him. The air was cool around him. The afternoon wind was rising. Treetops rustled.

He followed the trail to the meadow and trotted along its edge toward the cliff. He'd seen no sign that Nancarrow had more men, but there was always a chance. He stayed near the shelter of the trees.

At the cliff he started climbing. Once on top of the desolate plateau, he paused to catch his breath. Somewhere here they'd found Mr. Andrews' cap. That was where he'd probably been kidnapped. But why? It made no sense.

Pete glanced out over the panorama of forested mountains. The wind whipped across the granite and pierced his thin T-shirt. His jacket was tied around his waist and his space blanket was in his pocket. He'd need both later. He wished he'd taken the water bottle from Bob, but it was too late to go back for it now. At least he still had some of Jupe's candy bars.

He turned north, noting where the sun fell on his shoulder and back. The position of the sun was his only compass.

He moved uphill across the granite as it rose toward a stand of timber. At the wood's edge he looked for a trail. When he found none, he picked an opening through the trees and continued his trek north.

The land grew steep. He alternately fast-hiked and walked. The sun dipped lower toward the horizon. He continued to push his strong, athletic body. Sweat drenched him.

The terrain leveled and rose into hills again.

As the last of the day's light died, Pete stumbled up over a ridge and stopped. He stared down.

It was a miracle.

There was a dirt road running east and west. It was rutted like the Indians' road had been, but it was twice as wide. It looked just like the logging road Mary Grayleaf had described.

He slid down the ridge and stood quietly on the road for a moment, resting and savoring his success. Now if only a car would drive by and stop to help. . . .

His muscles throbbed. It had been a long hike. And he still had twenty-five, maybe thirty miles to go. With luck, he'd catch a ride once he reached the highway.

He turned west, heading into the last brilliant streaks of the setting sun. As he walked he pulled on his jacket. The temperature was dropping fast.

The sun set and the full moon rose. He hiked over a bridge that spanned the juncture of two fast-running streams. Mist filled the cold air. The scent of pine was heavy. He wished he dared drink the water.

On the other side of the bridge he paused. What looked like a forest service fire road branched left off the logging road. The fire road went downhill alongside the double stream. To keep trespassers out, there was a tubular gate with a shiny new padlock that reflected silver in the moonlight. The little road and fast stream continued south together, disappearing through a narrow gorge in the ridge that the swift water had carved out centuries ago.

At first Pete was excited that the forest service had a road here. Then he remembered that fire roads were often remote and were used infrequently—mostly to fight forest fires and make rescues. It was unlikely that the forest service would come out here unless they were notified of an emergency.

So Pete walked on. He ate his candy bars. He was growing more and more cold and tired. Coyotes howled across the mountains—the loneliest sound in the world.

◆ ◆ ◆

After leaving Pete, Bob and Jupe ran on, heavy feet pounding in hot pursuit after them. The pursuers came closer, and the guys increased their speed down the forest trail.

The sound was good news and bad news. The good news was that the three men must have passed Pete's hiding place without discovering Pete. The bad news was that now Bob and Jupe had to figure out a way to permanently lose the thugs and their M-16s.

Wordlessly, Bob and Jupe reached the stream the Indians called the Truoc, "the River." They headed upstream. The late afternoon wind was blowing over the clear, sparkling water toward them, carrying a sulfur smell that made their eyes burn.

Bob led, retracing the rocky path he'd followed the day before. They were out of breath and tired when they reached the talus-filled entrance to the Valley of the Ancestors. The dramatic waterfall roared down and then over the series of sparkling rapids.

"Wow!" Jupe exclaimed, staring up and up at the waterfall. "Is this where the landslide almost got you?"

"It was close," Bob said. He looked downstream. "There they are!"

Jupe followed his gaze. About half a mile away the three men were rounding a big boulder. Nancarrow was in the lead. They had their M-16s slung over their shoulders. They looked up and spotted the two guys. Biff, the short, runty one with the rough voice, shouted something and shook his fist.

"We'd better get out of here!" Jupe said.

Bob hurried back into the forest, following the cliff, with Jupe close behind. At last Bob stopped, reached up, and locked his fingers into almost invisible handholds. He stepped up onto almost invisible footholds. The holds had weathered so much over the centuries that they appeared to be natural crevices in the rock-face—until you looked closely.

Bob climbed.

Gingerly Jupe grabbed the first handholds and planted his feet into the narrow footholds. "Oh, boy," he breathed. He didn't like this. Sweat ran down his face and into his eyes. He balanced precariously.

"You can do it," Bob urged.

Bob climbed up the cliff, showing Jupe the way. Each step moved them higher and to the left—closer and closer to the sheer cliff above the waterfall. On the other side was the Valley of the Ancestors.

Tall trees blocked them from their pursuers' view. Not until Nancarrow and his men reached the rapids would they be able to see this section of the cliff, and by then the guys expected to be out of sight—safely in the Valley of the Ancestors.

Slowly Jupe moved his hands and feet from one set of holds to the next. His arms and legs trembled with the strain. *Why did I ever agree to this?* he asked himself. *I must be losing my mind!*

And then his right foot slid off its narrow ledge. It happened so quickly that he could do nothing. He was fifty feet above the ground, and the spray from the falls had made the granite slippery as ice. Before he could bring the foot back, his right hand started to slide.

Desperately he tried to hold on to the granite. His heart pounded. His fingers grabbed at the stone. But the more he tried to hold on, the more his right hand slipped. He stared at his hand—how could it be doing this! And then it slid off altogether.

Time seemed to stop.

Only his left hand and left foot were still in place. His body was out of control. Panting with fear, he swung out from the cliff like a door over the faraway ground. I'm going to die! he thought. I'm going to smash down on the rocks and die!

"Jupe!" Bob cried, stunned.

Jupiter's face was white. He seemed frozen.

"Dip your head!" Bob shouted. A hard fist of fear lodged in his chest. He had to save Jupe! "Move your right shoulder! Move your right leg. Change your balance so you'll swing back against the cliff!"

Jupe didn't move.

He hasn't heard me, Bob thought. "Jupe!" he bellowed. He reversed direction, crawling back down toward his friend.

Jupe sensed Bob. He didn't see Bob. He hardly heard him. But slowly Bob's directions were trickling through the muddle of Jupe's terrified mind. Use your head, Jupe told himself sternly. Think!

Just as Bob reached him, a look of deliberation came over Jupe's white face. Bob stared. He could almost see the wheels start to turn again in

Jupiter's great brain. Bob held his breath, hoping.

Suddenly Jupe's head jerked forward. His right shoulder twitched and followed his head. Next came his right leg.

Jupe swung back to the cliff. Like an overweight automaton, his hands and feet found their places. Exhausted, he leaned against the cliff.

"You did it, Jupe!" Bob called, excited. "You're okay! Now, come on. There's a ledge up here with some brush we can rest behind. They won't be able to see us. Come on, Jupe! It's not much farther!"

Stiffly, Jupe pried his hands loose. He reached for the next holds. His feet followed. With the same look of deliberation he moved up and across the cliff, jamming each hand and foot into its hold as if it were going to stay there for life.

Bob moved ahead. At last he scrambled up onto a narrow ledge. Thick spiny brush grew along the outer rim, drooping down the cliff face. It was a perfect cover.

"They're almost here!" Bob yelled. "Hurry!"

Jupe continued at the same slow pace. He never once looked around. He simply kept jamming his hands and feet into the holds until finally he was so close that Bob reached down and touched his fingers.

"You made it, Jupe," Bob said softly. Jupiter's fingers were icy cold.

Jupe said nothing. He shoved his hands and feet into the next crevices. Then he reached up and pulled himself onto the ledge next to Bob. He crawled behind the bushes. He sat still, closing his eyes.

"How close are they?" Jupe asked in a hoarse voice.

"Close enough," Bob said. "Look."

The cold mist from the waterfall swirled through the air, caught by the wind that whistled out of the valley. Sulfur stung their eyes as they gazed down at Nancarrow, Biff, and George hiking the last few steps to the waterfall.

"Where are those rotten jerks?" Nancarrow fumed. He stood hands on hips and surveyed the forest and cliffs through his wraparound sunglasses.

Bob and Jupe strained to hear his words over the roaring waterfall.

"You idiots let them get away!" Nancarrow shouted.

"They gotta be around here somewhere, boss!" George said.

"We'll find 'em!" Biff swore.

"We can't let them escape!" Nancarrow said angrily. "I've got that snoopy reporter Andrews safe. Now I've got to get my hands on those kids, too!"

At the mention of the word "reporter," Jupe and Bob looked at each other.

"It sounds like Nancarrow kidnapped your dad because he's a reporter investigating a story," Jupe said slowly. "Probably the story in Diamond Lake!"

"Poor Dad!" Bob said. "I wonder who MacKeir was, and what he knew."

"We've got to make it look accidental!" Nancarrow was still talking.

"We'll bang 'em on the head," Biff said. "Knock 'em out first like we did MacKeir!"

Bob and Jupe again looked at each other. They were shocked. Had Nancarrow's men killed MacKeir?

"Then put them into the plane," Oliver Nancarrow told him. "Burn them all up together—Andrews and the kids—make it look like it happened when the plane crashed. An accident just like MacKeir's. And no one will ever know the difference!"

"No one'll ever know!" Biff echoed fervently.

"You got it." Nancarrow patted him on the shoulder. "Now you head back, Biff. This may take a while. There's another shipment coming in tonight, and somebody's got to handle it. That somebody is you."

"Oh, boss," he said, disappointed.

"Do it right, and when I bring back the kids I'll let you take care of them yourself," Nancarrow promised.

Biff's face brightened. "O-*kay!*" He turned and trotted back down the stream.

"What shipment?" Bob wondered.

"Maybe the tip had to do with Nancarrow's shipments," Jupe said.

"Let's go, George," Nancarrow told his other underling. "Over this waterfall is a valley. Those kids might think that's a good place to hide."

Nancarrow started up the talus.

George grinned, showing all his crooked white teeth. He hugged his M-16 close and followed his boss toward the cliff just below where Jupiter and Bob hid.

The two Investigators froze. Once the thugs started up the slope, the guys would be exposed—with no other place to hide.

13

Valley of Death

BIG OLIVER NANCARROW AND HIS MAN GEORGE carefully crawled up over the loose rocks at the base of the cliff. Nancarrow spotted the same natural crevice that Bob had climbed up yesterday. He grabbed it, pulled himself up, and started up the cliff face.

"This don't look too safe," George muttered. He slung his M-16 across his back and followed.

They climbed steadily, their faces flushed and sweating. Unknowingly they were headed straight to the ledge where Jupiter and Bob were hiding.

"Jupe!" Bob whispered.

Jupiter's arms and legs were still very shaky, but his mind was working fine. He grabbed an exposed root next to the ledge. He tugged. Nothing happened. He pulled harder. The root snapped out of the cliff's crumbling face. Stones, dirt, and sand exploded out too.

Nancarrow and George looked up. The stones hurtled down. They gathered debris. Large rocks broke loose from the cliff and joined the landslide. Then boulders.

The two men scrambled away.

The rock slide thundered past.

"Boss . . ." George began. His tan hands trembled against the cliff.

"Forget it," Nancarrow said. "We'll go back. Those kids couldn't have made it through here. We'll camp at the stream tonight. Find them in the morning."

Bob let out a big sigh. "Thanks, Jupe."

Nancarrow and George picked their way back down the granite.

With Bob in the lead, the two guys continued their progress across the rockface. Soon the channel broadened. From above, they could see the lush green Valley of the Ancestors—at last.

The sun was beginning to set, casting long shadows across the width of the valley. The stream that ran down the center was wide, placid, and edged with tall grass. Every so often steam rose, probably from natural hot springs. The valley was so long they couldn't see the other end.

The guys kept moving.

Jupe looked at Bob. "Your eyes are red," he said. "Are mine?"

Bob looked closely, then nodded. "Just like the villagers'." He paused, thinking about what he'd said. "Hey, Daniel's eyes *weren't* red. He'd been away from the village for a day when we saw him. Maybe the *smell's* making them sick. They're downhill, right on the Truoc. The wind would funnel the stuff out of the valley and straight to them."

"They're pretty sick. It'd take more than the smell of sulfur for that." Jupiter spoke briefly. He was concentrating. He meticulously placed his hands and feet in the holds. He didn't grip too hard. Boy, did he want to get off this cliff! Slowly he descended. At last he stepped down into a mass of ferns and gave a huge sigh of relief. He was on terra firma again!

Jupe looked around. Some of the ferns and flowers, now that he saw them up close, were brown and wilted next to the stream. And the mostly sparkling-clear stream had a gray, scummy film caught in places against the bank.

"Hey, look at this scum," he said to Bob.

Bob looked down. "Gross. What is it?"

"Doesn't look natural, does it?" Jupe said.

"Maybe it's some kind of water pollution?"

"Yeah, maybe," Jupe said. "My eyes are burning. Let's get out of here."

The last golden rays of the sun disappeared behind the high valley rim. Cold, dark shadows settled over them. They put on their jackets and followed the stream, walking along the flat bank through thick, lush foliage that was brown and dying next to the water.

They were on a gentle incline. The other end of the valley was higher than this end. Occasional landslides had eroded parts of the valley's rock walls.

"You know, our plane crash was sure convenient," Jupe said thoughtfully. He took out a candy bar and began to eat.

"How so?" Bob asked. He drank from the water bottle and ate too.

"First the electrical system goes out," Jupe said, munching. "So we go down. And who happens to be nearby and wanting to kidnap your dad—Oliver Nancarrow!"

"Wow!" Bob's eyes widened. "You think he sabotaged the plane?"

"Him or one of his men."

The boys ate silently.

"What do we do now?" Bob said finally. "We've *got* to find Dad!"

In between chews Jupiter said, "Let's keep going. If I'm right, this valley runs south-north. And that means the logging road is ahead. Maybe we'll meet Pete there. Or the forest service!"

"Okay. At least Nancarrow won't come after us here. He doesn't want to climb the cliff."

"And maybe we can find out what's making the Indians sick," Jupe added.

They finished their candy bars and put the wrappers in their pockets. They'd carry them out to preserve the wilderness's ecology.

The valley was dark. Stars sparkled overhead. Slowly a full moon rose over the high rim.

Exhausted, they continued on in the moonlight, sometimes circling boulders and thick bushes before returning to the stream. After covering at least half a mile they had to swerve inland to avoid a marshy area. Skirting the ooze took them to the valley's wall. They had just turned back toward the river when Bob suddenly stopped, frozen to the spot. The hairs on the back of his neck stood on end.

"What's wrong?" Jupe asked quickly.

Wordlessly Bob pointed. About twenty feet ahead on the ground, something glowed eerily white.

Jupiter's heart pounded.

"Is it w-what I think it is?" Bob stammered.

Shoulder to shoulder, they walked slowly forward. As they got closer and could see more, the glow got larger and covered more area. Slivers of the pale light spilled through surrounding grass and bushes. The light wavered as the wind blew past.

At last Jupiter and Bob stopped. Bob trembled. Jupe tried to put on a brave front, but he was shaking too.

Close to their feet was a long, silvery bone. It was the one they'd first seen in the distance.

"L-look how long it is!" Bob managed.

"A tibia," Jupe got out. "Adult size. Looks like we found the Indians' cemetery!"

"I would've been just as happy to have missed it!" Bob said fervently. "Hey, a landslide must've unearthed these bones. How many are there, d'you think?" The bones were scattered over a big pile of dirt that had slid off the cliff next to them. Some of the bones stuck out from the ground.

"There's the other tibia," Jupe said. "And there's a femur and some ribs and pieces of the spine." The bones glowed with reflected light from the full moon. "It looks like a complete human skeleton!"

"There's the skull!" Bob said. "Creepy!"

Big black holes formed the skull's eyes. A small black triangle was where the nose had been. The jaw hung open in a perpetual toothy grin.

"Wait a minute!" Jupe said. He picked up something glittery. It was a silver belt buckle with a large turquoise stone embedded in the center.

Bob looked. "It's just like Daniel's!"

"His uncle's, maybe," Jupe said, putting the buckle in his pocket.

"But the uncle's been gone only a month. These bones . . ."

"Animals could have picked them clean."

Jupiter peered at the skull. He didn't feel scared anymore. He felt sick. And very, very sad. "Check this out." He pointed to a round hole through the skeleton's cranium.

"A bullet hole?"

"Yeah," Jupiter said unhappily. "Looks to me like someone murdered him."

◆ ◆ ◆

Pete walked on through the cold night, growing more and more tired. At last he stepped off the road and found a pine tree with thick, soft duff beneath. He wrapped his space blanket around him. Then he heard the sound of trucks. But they were heading in the wrong direction —back into the mountains from where he'd come.

Wearily he sat down. The trucks passed. Their lights were dimmed. Weird, Pete thought as he drifted off to sleep. Why drive with just parking lights?

He felt as if he'd slept hardly at all when he woke to the sound of trucks again. He looked at his digital watch. It was midnight.

He struggled to his feet. The trucks were headed the right way this time—toward the highway . . . and help for Mr. Andrews, Bob, and Jupiter!

He stumbled out onto the road. He waved the silvery space blanket back and forth over his head. The trucks lumbered toward him.

"Stop!" he yelled. "Stop!"

The lead truck slowed. The truck behind it slowed, too.

Excited, Pete ran up to the passenger side of the cab.

The first truck stopped. The door swung open to greet him.

He stepped on the running board and started to haul himself up into the cab.

Pete looked up. His gaze connected with the muzzle of an M-16 pointed straight at his forehead. Cold chills ran up and down his spine. He remembered Jupe's words about M-16s: "They're used for hunting people."

"Get in," runty little Biff growled. He gave a wolfish smile. "Where's your friends, boy?"

◆ ◆ ◆

Jupiter and Bob decided they needed to rest. They wrapped themselves in their space blankets and slept on a bed of ferns upstream from where they'd found the skeleton. They made no fire, figuring there was a chance Nancarrow or one of his men might spot it.

At dawn they were up and hiking. Their stomachs grumbled, but all they had was Jupe's raw popcorn kernels and no way to cook them. They looked longingly at plants and flowers, wondering whether they were edible. But they knew the old wilderness rule—if you don't know it, don't eat it. So they stayed hungry. Jupe reminded himself of all the weight he must be losing.

They walked steadily, keeping the stream on their left. There was no path, and the going was very slow. They passed sulfur-reeking hot springs, held their breath, and ran by. Every so often they passed a patch of gray scum or multicolored oil swirling down the water.

At last they topped a rise.

They paused, feeling the first flush of hard-won success. Spread ahead was the other end of the valley, green and luminous in the noonday sun. The valley was very wide. It ended in an upward-sloping tree-dotted ridge through which the stream rushed toward them.

"A road!" Bob said, pushing his cap back on his head.

A little dirt road also entered the upper end of the valley through the stream's deep, narrow gorge. The road had been built on a lip just above the far side of the stream. The road continued toward them for several hundred yards and then ended in a flat, hard-packed dirt circle—a turnaround circle.

"That doesn't look like the logging road Mary Grayleaf described," Bob said.

"Nothing like it," Jupe agreed.

They waded across the stream. An awful stench arose. They held their breath and looked down. A black tarlike substance had been caught in little pools along the stream. The vegetation around the pools was dead or dying.

They studied the placid water. It was murky and the oil slick reflected a rainbow of colors on the surface.

Quickly the guys moved on, gasping for air.

"It looks a lot like oil or asphalt, or maybe both," Bob said.

"And it stinks a lot worse."

"Hey, it reminds me of that foul mess you brewed in chem lab," Bob said, making a face.

"That happened to be a complex thermo-reactive experiment," Jupe began huffily, but then he chuckled. "Remember what a fit Mr. Perry had when it blew up and splattered all over the ceiling?"

The two guys roared with laughter as they walked onto the hard-packed dirt turnaround. There were many tire tracks.

"Trucks," Bob said. He reached down and picked up a cigarette butt just like the ones Jupe had found.

Jupe nodded grimly. "Delivering 'shipments,' I bet."

"Nancarrow Trucking Company! Maybe Dad is around here somewhere!"

The two studied the polluted stream, the brush, the

trees, and the ridge. Another narrow road branched off from the turnaround heading northwest as it disappeared into a wooded area of pines and birches.

"Look over there," Jupiter said.

On the southwest side of the turnaround was a series of natural caves low on the ridge. Tire tracks led across the flatlands to the caves. The guys hustled over.

"Dad?" Bob called. His mouth was dry with excitement.

They walked down the line of cave openings, but the eye-burning odor coming out of the caves was too much for them. They coughed, wheezed, and returned to where they started.

"This one doesn't smell too bad," Jupe decided, looking into the cave nearest the road.

They peered into the shadowy interior.

"I see square shapes," Bob said.

They entered and paused for their eyes to adjust to the dimness. Sunlight streamed in through the large round opening.

At last they could see. They looked around in awe. Stacked from the dirt floor to the rocky ceiling were hundreds of 55-gallon drums.

Jupe read a label. "PCBs," he said.

Bob read another. "Acids."

Jupe explored. "Alkalines, oxidizers, sulfur sludge."

The guys stared at each other in horror.

"Toxic wastes," Jupe stated.

"We've found a hazardous materials dump," Bob said.

Suddenly darkness enveloped them.

They looked up at the cave's entrance. A man's dark, menacing silhouette filled the opening.

They were trapped!

14

Dirty Business

"JUPITER! BOB!" THE VOICE CALLED ANGRILY INTO the cave. "What are you doing here!"

The guys looked at each other.

"Daniel?" Jupiter asked.

"How'd you know it was us?" Bob said.

Daniel was growing angrier. "Get out of there! This is forbidden. You're in our sacred valley!"

"No!" Jupe countered. "*You come in here.* We'll show you what's making your tribe sick!"

Daniel hesitated. He stepped into the cave.

"Give your eyes time to adjust," Jupe warned.

"This better be good," Daniel said.

"It is," Jupe promised. He showed their new friend the barrels. At the back of the cave one had begun to leak onto the dirt floor. Quickly they moved away from the burning fumes and outdoors into the sun. Jupiter explained what the 55-gallon drums contained.

"Toxic wastes?" Daniel said. "Poisoning our air and water?"

"Your eyes are red again," Bob said. "Now ours are too."

Daniel looked at the two guys. "Then the Truoc is probably not safe for drinking. Or the fish safe for eating."

"The animals you hunt drink the water too," Bob reminded him.

"The other caves smelled so bad that we couldn't even go inside," Jupiter said. "They must be full of leaking drums."

Daniel looked grim, thinking about the quantity and the danger of the toxic materials. And then he looked furious. "Who would do this to our sacred valley?"

"Oliver Nancarrow," Jupe said simply. "Of Nancarrow Trucking Company. Know him?"

"Of course," Daniel said. "Our headman works for him sometimes. But Mr. Nancarrow helps our village. . . ."

"He also hangs out around *here*," Bob said. "If Nancarrow kidnapped my dad, where would he be?"

"I don't know," Daniel said. "I've never been in this end of the valley. But I'll bet we can track him—or Mr. Nancarrow."

As they walked back to the turnaround Jupiter asked, "Is that how you found us—by tracking?"

Daniel moved hunched over, his eyes studying the multitude of tire prints. "Grandfather released me from the singing way ceremony early this morning," he said as he paused to examine thick treads. "He was worried about you. So I borrowed Aunt's truck and found the broken-down pickup. Your shoes have patterned soles, and they're easy to follow. There were first two, then three pairs of hiking boots chasing you. You ran, had two fights, and then you guys separated from Pete. Pete got away, I think, but the boots kept after you."

"You could tell all that?" Jupiter asked, amazed.

"I know the forest," Daniel said simply. "And Uncle taught me to track."

"Did your tracking tell you who sabotaged the pickup?" Jupe said.

"What?" Daniel asked, shocked.

Jupe explained about the bolt that had been cut behind the brake pedal.

Daniel bowed his head. "Who could've done such a terrible thing?" He looked up. "I'm glad you're all right. Pete must be a great driver."

The two Investigators nodded.

"Uh . . ." Bob said, looking at Jupe.

Jupe nodded somberly. There was no way to soften the next question. "Daniel, tell us if you recognize this," Jupe said, holding out his hand. On it was the silver belt buckle with the turquoise stone embedded in the center.

Silently Daniel took the buckle. It was almost identical to the one he wore. "It's my uncle's." He looked up. "Where did you find it?"

"Back down the valley, next to the skeleton," Jupe

said. "You must have seen the bones on your way up here."

Daniel closed his eyes and nodded. His jaw tightened and then relaxed.

"Now I know what my vision quest message meant," he whispered. " 'In the right place, but without blessing.' Uncle's body is in the sacred valley, but his spirit hasn't been blessed from this life into the next."

The three of them were quiet a moment.

"Did you stop to look at the bones?" Jupe asked softly.

"I was too worried about you," Daniel said.

"Then I have more bad news. There was a bullet hole through his skull."

"He was shot?" Daniel said, stunned. "Who? Why?"

Bob told Daniel about the "accidental" death of Mark MacKeir and of Nancarrow's intention to kill Mr. Andrews and the Three Investigators.

"You think Uncle found . . . this?" Daniel waved his arm, encompassing the deadly caves and the road over which the toxic wastes were transported.

"Could be," Jupiter said.

Daniel thought a moment. "Grandfather learned in the ceremony that a foreign witch was making us sick. He said the witch was filled with greed, and only by giving the witch what it wants can it be destroyed."

"Nancarrow must be the witch," Jupe said.

"But what does it mean—give the witch what it wants?" Bob asked, puzzled.

"I don't know," Daniel told them. He put his uncle's belt buckle in his pocket. "Let's find out." He pointed down at the set of wide tire tracks in the dirt. "That's Mr. Nancarrow's Winnebago." He trotted off, following the treads.

Jupiter and Bob hustled after him, astounded by what Daniel could deduce from the multitude of unclear marks in the dirt. They ran along the narrow dirt drive that curved away from the turnaround, up through thick pines and birches. Once out of sight of the caves, they slowed, proceeding cautiously.

Soon the scent of pine replaced the stench from the caves.

Daniel stopped. "There it is. Mr. Nancarrow's Winnebago. He drives it to the village sometimes to bring us presents—food, ammunition, toys for the kids."

The large, luxurious recreational vehicle was parked in an open area where the drive ended. It was out of sight of the caves and protected from the toxic fumes by the trees.

Daniel started for it.

"Wait!" Jupiter said. "Maybe somebody's there. Those guys are carrying M-16s!"

Daniel pointed to prints in the dirt. Diamond shapes filled the soles. The prints headed toward the RV.

"Do you recognize who's here?" Daniel asked.

Jupiter and Bob shook their heads.

"Pete. Everyone else has left. See the boot marks?" He pointed to other prints leaving the RV.

"They got Pete!" Jupiter cried.

They stared at Daniel, astonished and suddenly even more worried.

"Let's go!" Daniel said.

"But be careful," Jupe warned. "Nancarrow could be nearby."

Stooped over, the three guys ran quietly to the RV. When they reached it, they stood up slowly and peered through the windows. There were two figures inside. Pete was gagged and tied to a metal kitchen chair. Someone else was tied next to him.

"Dad!" Bob shouted.

15

Death Trap

JUPITER AND BOB PULLED OFF THE GAGS SILENCING Mr. Andrews and Pete.

"Dad, are you okay?" Bob cried.

"I am now," Mr. Andrews said with feeling. The bruise on his forehead was still enormous and the wound was fiery red. He needed a doctor. Bob promised himself that they would find one as soon as—if—they escaped this mess.

"How'd they get you, Pete?" Jupiter wanted to know as he untied Pete. The tall Investigator looked exhausted.

"I was tired and stupid and got caught," Pete said, simplifying the situation considerably. "Biff knew a trail through the woods. He beat me to the road, and collected his wheels."

Once free, Mr. Andrews and Pete stood up, moving their stiff arms and legs.

"Thanks, fella," Mr. Andrews said cheerfully as he removed his blue Dodgers cap from Bob's head.

"My pleasure," Bob said, grinning happily at his father. Then he remembered to introduce Daniel.

Pete recovered quickly, did a few leg pumps, and headed for the RV's refrigerator. "I'm starved," he announced, pulling out peanut butter and bread and juice. Everyone dived on the food.

Mr. Andrews continued to walk around the cramped RV, holding on to shelves and to the backs of chairs. "Thank goodness you guys are all right. Tell me what's happened while I've been"—he gestured at the kitchen chair and smiled grimly—"tied up."

Bob related their adventures and discoveries of the last two days. "Mark MacKeir's dead, Dad," Bob finished. "Nancarrow killed him."

"Actually," Mr. Andrews said, "I believe Biff did the dirty work. He'd been tailing Mark and knew he was going to meet me. George sabotaged the Cessna's electrical system to get rid of me. He planted a tiny explosive on an important cluster of wires behind the cabin's fire wall."

"He must've installed an electronic fuse, too," Jupe mused with his mouth full. "That way Nancarrow could trigger the bomb from the ground."

"Line of sight," Mr. Andrews confirmed. "Nancarrow wanted to bring me down where he could be sure I was dead. I'd filed a flight plan, so he knew where to expect me. If I survived, all the better. Then he could find out if I'd told anyone about the story. When he discovered more people were involved—you guys—he was terrified. He had a nice half-million-dollar-a-year illegal operation thriving here and couldn't afford an investigation."

"He makes that much money storing hazardous chemicals?" Pete asked, astounded.

"You bet," Mr. Andrews said, "and he's small time. Why do you think companies all over the nation are being fined by the Environmental Protection Agency? Legal disposal is necessary but costly. Some companies will do anything to save the money and hassle. Just a couple of weeks ago, the EPA caught one Los Angeles business pouring lethal liquids straight into the city sewers."

"Wow," Jupe said. "That means sewage plant workers, landfills, and agricultural water could be contaminated."

"Exactly," Mr. Andrews said. "After that incident, the city editor assigned me to start research for a series on hazardous waste. That's when Mark MacKeir called the newspaper and asked to talk to a reporter. At first he was so terrified of what might happen if he talked that he wouldn't give me his name. All he said was that he worked for a chain of auto body shops and had discovered the owner was cutting costs by paying somebody shady to cart the waste away, no questions asked. You know, stuff like brake fluid, transmission fluid, drained motor oil, paint thinner. When the owner wouldn't stop it and threatened to fire MacKeir, he followed the trucker—Nancarrow—and found his operation. MacKeir was a decent man who wanted illegal dumps to be publicized so people would understand how dangerous toxic wastes could be. That's why he agreed to show me what was going on."

Daniel had been leaning against the door, listening quietly. "They're ruining our valley," he said. "The land, the water, the animals, even the air we breathe. They're making all of us sick, and maybe they killed my uncle, too."

"The government knows a lot about toxic cleanup," Mr. Andrews said. "They'll do what they can. I'm sorry about your uncle's death. I didn't hear any of them talk about him, so I don't know what happened or whether they did it."

Jupiter moved to the front of the RV. He sat in the driver's seat. "Mr. Andrews, do you have enough information for your story?"

"I've got a good start," Mr. Andrews said. "A lot of Nancarrow's records are in his desk right here, just waiting for me to read. The RV is his office. Being on the move all the time makes him harder to catch."

"Then let's split," Pete said. "We'll take the office with us. Jupe, move over." Pete headed for the front. "I'll drive."

"No, I'll drive," Mr. Andrews said, following Pete.

"You're too sick, Mr. Andrews," Pete said.

"He's right, Dad," Bob said.

"I'm fine," Mr. Andrews said. He frowned, sud denly dizzy. He grabbed the back of a chair, ther down. "Maybe you've got a point," he admitt

"I can't find the keys," Jupiter said. "Do you know where they are, Mr. Andrews?"

"Nancarrow must have them."

The guys' hearts fell.

"Okay. I'll jump-start it," Pete said. He headed for the door so he could work under the hood.

"Wait." Daniel's voice turned distant, commanding. He was as unmoving as he'd been in the forest when Pete had caught him. He closed his eyes, listening through the RV's open window. "There are men out there."

Quickly the five dropped down and peered over the window sills. Daniel was right. They could make out movement through the pines and birches. Movement all around the clearing. A shadowy form sometimes. Other times the mirrorlike flash of sunlight reflected from gunmetal.

"It's an ambush!" Jupiter told them, breathing hard.

The others gulped.

"I see Nancarrow!" Mr. Andrews whispered suddenly.

"And that bloodthirsty pipsqueak Biff," Pete added.

"That guy is dangerous," Bob said nervously. "He *likes* to hurt people."

"Hey, I see our headman," Daniel said, surprised. "And Ike Ladysmith."

"Ike Ladysmith works for the headman?" Jupe asked, recognizing the wiry guy as the one who had signaled Mary that the pickup was ready.

"Sometimes," Daniel said. "Look, the headman

and Ike have walkie-talkies! And new rifles. I didn't know anyone in the village had such fine equipment! Our headman is an amazing shot. For him a rifle is the greatest gift of all."

"Ruger 10/22 hunting rifles," Jupe identified them. He had a moment of panic. How were they going to get out of here when they were surrounded with high-powered weapons?

"Mary said your headman's been buying things for the village," Bob added. "Expensive things like new motor parts. And then there's his brand-new red pickup. Maybe all his new wealth has just been money Nancarrow's been paying him to keep quiet about this place."

Daniel's handsome face turned dark and stormy with disbelief. "No! He's an honorable man!"

Tension mounted in the RV. Daniel's anger inside was almost as bad as Nancarrow's threat outside.

"The situation doesn't look good," Mr. Andrews said diplomatically, "but Daniel's right. We don't have enough evidence to accuse the headman . . . or Ike Ladysmith, either."

"Then who loused up the brakes and almost killed us?" Pete asked.

Daniel stared at him a moment, then turned away. "I don't know," he said quietly.

"Well," Jupe said, again heading for the driver's seat, "I know one thing. We'd better figure a way out of here—pronto."

"Any guns in this thing?" Pete asked, searching a tiny broom closet.

"Forget it," Mr. Andrews said. "Nancarrow keeps his M-16 with him. We have to think of another way."

Jupiter was running his hand under the dashboard and his mind was racing a mile a minute. "If Aunt Mathilda taught me one thing, it's to be prepared. And a guy like Nancarrow has to be really prepared, especially when this RV is his office. . . . Aha!" Jupe brought his hand out from under the dashboard. Dramatically he opened his hand to reveal a little magnetic case—the kind people store their extra car keys in. "Can you imagine his trying to make a fast getaway when he left his keys in his other pants?"

The tension in the little RV eased for a moment. Triumphantly Jupe handed the case to Pete. Pete got into the driver's seat.

"Okay, Pete," Mr. Andrews said. He sat down again, weak. "Take her out the way Biff brought you in. Just follow the road. If they blow the tires, keep going. Don't let *anything* stop you. We're headed for Diamond Lake!"

Bob looked quickly at his father when he heard the urgency in his voice. Mr. Andrews didn't show fear often—but this was one of those times.

Pete nodded. "Everybody down. Hold on to something."

The three guys and Mr. Andrews hit the floor of the RV. Daniel lay tense, his senses super alert. Bob wondered if he'd ever see Jennifer again, or Amy, or Debbie. . . . Jupe gulped and prayed they'd have better luck with the RV than with the Ford pickup.

And Pete took a deep breath and turned on the ignition. The motor roared to life.

16

Destroying the Witch

THE RV TURNED. PETE DROVE, HUNCHED OVER THE steering wheel, as small a target as possible. In one swift moment they rounded the clearing. He glimpsed astonishment on Oliver Nancarrow's broad face.

Then bullets thudded into the RV. They whined through one side and exited through the other.

"Everyone okay back there?" Pete yelled.

"Okay!" four voices shouted back.

More bullets hit the RV while others bit into the road and showered dust and dirt clods into the air.

Pete sped the RV toward the little drive that wound out through the birches and pines.

The grim, sturdy headman appeared at Oliver Nancarrow's side, enraged and talking. Nancarrow listened and swung an arm in signal for his men to stop firing. He picked his walkie-talkie from his belt and spoke.

As the RV raced past Nancarrow he did a strange thing—he smiled nastily at the speeding vehicle. Pete couldn't figure it. They were escaping. Why would Nancarrow smile?

"They're letting us go!" Pete called back to his friends.

The RV roared down the narrow, winding road, Pete's foot pressed as far down on the accelerator as he dared. Because of the curves, he couldn't see more than twenty-five feet ahead. The RV rocked from side to side, brushing pine branches.

And then he saw the reason for Nancarrow's nasty smile. Pete slammed on the brakes.

"What's going on?" someone shouted from the back.

Ahead was a large Nancarrow company truck, parked across the narrow road just where it opened into the turnaround. George or someone must have arrived to deliver a shipment. There was no way Pete could get the big RV—or even a little Volkswagen bug—around it. The truck was bumper to bumper with the trees.

"We're trapped!" Pete yelled.

The RV screeched to a halt. Nancarrow's man George stepped out from behind the truck, his M-16 pointed at Pete, his walkie-talkie swinging from his belt.

The RV's four passengers pulled themselves up to the windows.

"What're we gonna do now?" Bob groaned.

Jupe started pinching his lower lip.

"Get out here, wise guys!" George bellowed at

them. "I'm gonna let you live a little longer only 'cause the boss said so!"

"Nancarrow and his men will be here soon," Mr. Andrews warned the others.

"I've got an idea," Jupe said quietly. "I'll distract George, and you guys pile out and take off."

"Move it, dipsticks!" George roared outside.

"Be careful!" Mr. Andrews urged.

Jupe nodded. He grabbed the handle of the door and paused. Then he took a deep breath and he opened the door. He put his hands to his head, holding the sides and squinting in mock pain.

"Ohhhhh!" he moaned as he staggered out the door. "Ohhhhh, I'm so sick!" He stumbled and staggered toward George.

George frowned. He cocked his head in suspicion. He moved the M-16 so that it covered Jupiter.

"I'm gonna die with the pain!" Jupe cried, stumbling onward. "Help me!"

"Get away!" George yelled.

Jupiter flung up his arm and "accidentally" pushed aside the M-16. "Help me!" He threw himself with despair at George.

"Blast it!"

Pete barreled out the RV's door, followed by Bob, Daniel, and Mr. Andrews.

Jupe and George collapsed to the ground, Jupe on top.

"Get off me, you fat slob!" George snarled as he tried to slide out from under Jupiter's bulk.

"They're getting away!" Nancarrow shouted from the road. "Stop them!"

Nancarrow and his men thundered toward them.

Jupiter jumped to his feet. Bob and Mr. Andrews fled into the woods. Pete raced across the dirt turn-around toward the road that led out of the valley. Daniel raced like the wind to the cab of another Nancarrow company truck. And Jupiter headed after Pete.

But the village's headman was hot after Jupiter, closing in quickly. Jupe veered off, pounding toward the caves. He had another idea. He remembered how angry the headman had been at Nancarrow a moment ago.

Jupiter ran into the first toxic waste cave. The headman was right behind.

"Come out of there!" Amos Turner said angrily as he entered. "You have caused enough trouble. No one belongs in the sacred valley!"

"What about Nancarrow and his men?" Jupe retorted.

"They help our people! The Creator would understand. Our villagers have hard lives. Since Mr. Nancarrow rented this end of the valley, things are better!"

"The sickness hasn't made anything better."

"That has nothing to do with Mr. Nancarrow," the grim headman insisted. "Now come on out!"

"Look at these barrels," Jupe continued. "Smell the fumes? They're filled with toxic wastes—*poisons.*"

The headman looked at the stacks of drums. He shook his head. "Mr. Nancarrow said he was storing explosives here. My job is to let him know when strangers come onto the reservation. He has competitors who will stop at nothing to take his business away. That is why he asked me to keep the rental, and even the walkie-talkies, secret. If he wants to store other things here too, that is none of my business." The headman paused, then said stubbornly, "His rent is important. It makes life easier for my people!"

"But the toxic wastes are making them sick!"

The headman walked around Jupiter, pointed his Ruger rifle at Jupe's back, and snapped out, "Go!"

"Nancarrow is the witch," Jupiter told him as he walked through the cave's opening into the sunlight. "And I don't believe you really want to hurt me."

For a moment the headman hesitated. Then he thrust his Ruger once more at Jupiter and herded him toward the turnaround where Nancarrow waited.

In the forest Ike Ladysmith patiently tracked Bob and Mr. Andrews. He would find them eventually.

Pete and Biff fought near the stream. Pete couldn't seem to get the M-16 away from him.

"Nephew!" the headman called to Daniel.

Daniel was frantically trying to start the second truck. George had flung open the cab door and trained his M-16 on him.

"Stop that foolishness!" the headman told Daniel. "Come here now!"

Jupe saw that he and his friends were trapped. It was

only a matter of time before Nancarrow would order his men to shoot Mr. Andrews and the guys. Finding out whether the guys had told anyone would no longer be worth the trouble.

With them out of the way, Nancarrow would go on polluting the valley and making the village sick. The Indians would continue looking for a witch they would never find. There would be more singing ceremonies and more messages.

Messages! During the ceremony the singing doctor had given Daniel a message: Give the witch what it wants and it will be destroyed.

Jupiter looked around. If Nancarrow was the witch, what he wanted was to capture everyone. Jupe thought about that, and slowly an idea began to form. It was a terrible risk . . . but they had no choice.

"Daniel! Pete! Bob! Mr. Andrews!" Jupe shouted. "Come over here. Give up!"

"Forget it!" Pete bellowed. Just then wiry Biff slammed the butt of his M-16 into Pete's stomach and knocked the wind out of him.

"No way!" Daniel said. But then Daniel realized that George's M-16 was aimed right at his heart.

Ike Ladysmith pounced in the bushes. He stood up, pulling Mr. Andrews up by the collar of his Windbreaker. Bob rose next to him.

"Come on, guys!" Jupe yelled. "We have to give up!"

Puzzled and angry, they moved toward the dirt turnaround. Nancarrow's men followed warily.

"You know Nancarrow's going to kill us," Jupe told the headman.

"He will simply throw you off our reservation," the headman said, still thinking Jupiter was exaggerating.

"Just like he had you sabotage the pickup's brakes?"

"What?" the headman asked. "I saw the pickup where you had crashed it, but I did not . . ." His broad, grim face was suddenly lined with doubt.

When everyone had gathered in the turnaround, Jupiter pointed to Daniel's unusual silver belt buckle. "Do you know anyone else who has a buckle like that?" he asked the headman.

"Daniel's uncle," the headman said.

Daniel took his uncle's buckle from his pocket and handed it to the headman. "Jupiter found it down the valley," he said, "lying next to a skeleton. The skeleton had a bullet hole through its skull."

Biff froze. He turned to Nancarrow and yelled, "I told you we should've killed these guys right away just like we did the old Indian!"

Biff ran for the truck.

"Come back, you little coward!" Nancarrow shouted.

Before Nancarrow could move, the headman raised his new Ruger. A shot rang out.

Biff's M-16 flew from his hands, shot away by the headman's bullet. Pete tore after Biff.

The headman swung around, taking aim at Nancarrow.

"Wait a minute!" Nancarrow pleaded, dropping his M-16 and backing off.

"You killed my cousin!" the headman raged at Oliver Nancarrow, walking toward the frightened crook. "And now you would kill these innocent people!" He slammed the gun into Nancarrow's belly.

Nancarrow doubled up. The headman smashed his fist up into Nancarrow's jaw. For a moment Nancarrow looked surprised. Then his eyes closed and he toppled backward, unconscious.

Bob karate-kicked high. His foot connected with George's chin. He pivoted, gave another *mae-geri* kick, and George collapsed onto Nancarrow.

Pete grabbed Biff by the arm and spun him around. While the runty guy was off balance, Pete slammed a hard *mae hiji-ate* forearm into his chest.

"No! Stop!" Biff wheezed. He raised his hands. "Please! I give up! I only did what Ollie said. I swear!"

With a disgusted grimace, Pete prodded Biff back to the others.

"I am in your debt," Amos Turner said slowly to the Three Investigators. "I did not want to believe that Mr. Nancarrow could be so evil."

"He did a great job of pretending to help your village," Mr. Andrews said.

"And it's actually the singing doctor you are indebted to," Jupe said, and explained how the shaman's message had helped him.

Daniel gazed around the clearing. "Where's Ike?"

Like a ghost, Ike Ladysmith had disappeared into the forest.

"Nancarrow must have been paying him on the side," the headman told Daniel. "It had to be Ike who tampered with the pickup's brakes. He almost killed your friends."

Daniel said, "Then he's trying to escape."

"I will find him," the headman said with finality. "Now we must tie up these others and put them in a truck. . . ."

"In the RV, please," Mr. Andrews said. "There are important documents inside that the police should see. We can drive the whole lot into Diamond Lake at the same time."

"Of course," the headman said agreeably. "The RV. Daniel will go with you. He will show you where the police station is."

"What about Ike?" Pete wanted to know.

"We have our own reservation police," the headman said.

"Uncle is the chief of police," Daniel explained.

"Part of our treaty with the United States government is that we take care of our own crime," the headman said. "Reservations are entitled to that. We also prosecute our own criminals."

"Grandfather is the judge," Daniel added, to no one's surprise.

They tied up Nancarrow and his two thugs and put them in the back of the RV. Turner moved the big truck out of the way. As Pete drove out, heading toward the logging road, the headman waved. He was smiling at last.

The headman leaped from the truck, walked lightly away, and disappeared into the forest.

◆ ◆ ◆

Daniel directed them into Diamond Lake, following the route his sister Mary had described what now seemed eons ago—but was just the day before.

As they drove into the little resort town they passed glistening swimming pools, a golf course, regulation tennis courts, Western-saddle riders on prancing horses, hikers with bright backpacks, walkers in designer sportswear, handsome lodges, and luxurious hotels. A big Learjet roared overhead into the private airstrip.

"Right on target," Pete sighed. "Guys, we made it at last."

"I'm starved," Jupiter announced.

"I need a telephone," Mr. Andrews said, "and a bath."

"And a doctor," Bob added, smiling.

Three girls standing on the corner noticed Bob's magnetic smile. They waved and whistled at him.

Daniel looked puzzled. "Girls whistle at Bob? Isn't it supposed to be the other way around?"

"Gee, what can I say, guys?" Bob asked, giving them the same dynamite smile.

Pete turned from the steering wheel and pitched one of the RV cushions at him.

Jupe jumped on top of him.

"You know," Daniel told him thoughtfully, his handsome face solemn, "the singing doctor could cast an enchantment on you, and relieve you of the terrible responsibility of your appeal. . . ."

"No, no! Stop!" Bob laughed. "Jupe! Get off! You may have lost weight, but not that much. No enchantments! Please. I'll get you *all* dates!"

"Good," Jupe said, rising, "and we'll describe the case to them in complete detail. I'm sure the girls would like to know how the Sierras were formed. In fact, did you know *sierra* means 'mountain range' in Spanish? So when you say the Sierra mountains, you're saying the Mountain Range mountains. . . ."

Everyone else groaned as Pete pulled up to the Diamond Lake police station.

Funny Business

First published in a single volume in paperback in
the USA in 1989 Random House, Inc
First published in paperback in 1990 in Armada

1

Comix!

"WHAT THE. . . ?" JUPITER JONES LOOKED UP FROM THE car engine he was supposed to be working on. He straightened quickly, nearly cracking his head on the hood of the old white Chevy Impala. As the founder of The Three Investigators, Jupe was a keen, cool-headed observer. But even a 17-year-old detective can be left gawking sometimes.

Uncle Titus had just returned from a collecting trip. Titus Jones was famous for coming up with the world's strangest salvage. His finds dotted the grounds of The Jones Salvage Yard. From the auto grease pit Jupe could see some of them—the herd of carousel horses, the clump of candy-striped barber poles. But from the look of things, this time Uncle Titus had outdone himself.

Sitting behind the wheel of the yard's large collection truck, Jupe's uncle wore a fur cap with a raccoon tail down the back. In the back of the pickup Hans and Konrad were trying out hula hoops.

Jupe brushed back his dark brown hair, his eyes

wide with disbelief at the spectacle. As he eased his stocky frame around the Impala's hood to see what his aunt would make of all this his elbow struck a can of motor oil. It began glugging its contents into the crankcase.

"Oof!" A thump came from under the chassis. Jupe's pal Pete Crenshaw shot out from below the car. "You're not supposed to pour until I put the plug back in!"

Pete was a tall, athletic guy, one of Jupe's associates in The Three Investigators detective agency. He didn't look his best lying on a wheeled mechanic's board, sputtering from a mouthful of fresh oil. The stuff had also plastered down his reddish-brown hair.

The idea had been to drain the old oil out of Pete's latest used car and put some new lubricant into the engine. But that was before Jupe's oil spill.

Jupe grabbed for the now empty can. "Sorry," he apologized. "I got—distracted."

"By what? World War III?" Then Pete caught sight of Jupe's Aunt Mathilda. The tall, heavyset woman was marching toward the truck. "Uh-oh. Maybe that's exactly what it will be."

"Titus Jones," Aunt Mathilda burst out. "Where did you find this, this"—she waved her arms helplessly—"this *junk*?"

"It isn't junk," Uncle Titus protested. "It's prime salvage material. Collector's items."

"Like that silly hat on your head?"

Uncle Titus flicked the fur tail. "It's a genuine Davy Crockett coonskin cap."

Aunt Mathilda quickly walked to the back of the truck. "Collector's items, my foot. Hula hoops. Pogo sticks. And what's in this trunk?" She flipped up the heavy top and sucked in her breath. "Comic books! You actually spent money for this?"

Although Jupe was overweight, he could move fast when he wanted to. Now he hurried over to the pickup for a look. Inside the trunk, just as his aunt had said, were mounds and mounds of comics.

"Wow!" Pete muttered beside him. "This guy must have really loved comics."

"They look pretty old," Jupe said. "Those books must have been tucked away for years." He turned to Pete. "How much money do you have on you?"

"Not a lot." Pete began digging through his pockets.

"Hey, guys, what's up?" Bob Andrews asked, grinning. The tall, blond third Investigator had just walked in through the salvage yard gate. He looked tanned and trim in a white polo shirt and pleated khaki pants. Jupe was almost surprised to find him alone. Ever since Bob had replaced his glasses with contact lenses, a fan club of girls could be expected to be tagging after him—if they weren't hanging around the junkyard waiting for him to show up.

Now Jupe pounced on him. "How much money have you got?"

Bob reached into his pocket. "You're catching me at a bad time. What do you need it for?"

Jupe grinned. "I want to buy some comics."

Up on the truck Aunt Mathilda was still poking

through the contents of the trunk. "They may be valuable. But how do we find out? And where will we find buyers?"

"Right here." Jupe snatched the money from Bob and Pete, adding it to the bills he'd found in his own pockets. "I have . . ." He counted quickly. "Twenty-one dollars and seventeen cents. We'll undertake all the worry and work. How about it, Aunt M?"

"Done!" Aunt Mathilda grabbed the money. Uncle Titus looked as if he were about to argue. Then he saw the look in his wife's eyes.

But Jupe got a lot of argument from his friends as they unloaded the trunk.

"You borrowed our money to buy *this*?" Bob grunted as they swung the big box down.

"Jupe's losing it," Pete said. "First he pours motor oil all over my face and now he pulls this."

"Motor oil, huh?" Bob leaned toward Pete's head and sniffed. "I thought you were using some new kind of hair-styling stuff."

"If you two have finished clowning around," Jupe said, "I'll explain about your brilliant investment."

"*Our* investment?" Bob asked, frowning.

"You'll see your money several times over." Jupe tapped the trunk. "Depending on what we find inside."

"That junk?" Pete's voice was disbelieving.

"Buried treasure," Jupe insisted. "Do you know what some of those old comics go for? Some are worth thousands of dollars."

"*Thousands* . . . ?" Bob stared at the trunk.

"Of course, we don't know what's in there," Jupe went on. "We may find only a few hundred dollars' worth." He rubbed his hands together. "My hope is that the proceeds will be enough for me to buy a car. Whatever there is, we'll divide it three ways. Agreed?"

◆ ◆ ◆

The next Friday afternoon the Investigators were in Pete's Impala, heading toward downtown Los Angeles. For once, all three guys had the weekend free. Pete's girlfriend, Kelly Madigan, had gone away to cheerleaders' camp. Bob had a few days off from his part-time job at Sax Sendler's Rock-Plus talent agency. And Jupe could call his time his own now that he'd computerized the junkyard inventory for Aunt Mathilda.

Pete glared in the rear-view mirror at the trail of smoke the Impala left behind. "You know, Jupe, we're still burning oil from that can you spilled all over the engine," he grumbled. "And I swear I can still smell that gunk on my hair."

"At least you're not half-blind from going through all those stupid comics," Bob said. "Sorting out those books while Jupe figured out how much they were worth was worse than my old library job."

"I think having all those comics is kind of neat," said Pete. "You know, I remember reading some of them when I was a little kid. The Crimson Phantom . . ." He shook his head and sighed. "He was my all-time favorite."

"You can afford to be nostalgic," Bob complained. "You were out with Kelly most of the time we were working. Jupe's too chicken to try interrupting *her* social life." Kelly Madigan had not only efficiently staked out Pete as her boyfriend—she'd just as firmly staked out most of his spare time as well.

In the back, Bob shot a dirty look at the cardboard box on the floor. "So I got stuck digging through this junk." He gave the box of comics a kick.

"Careful," Jupe said, turning in his seat. "You don't want to damage the merchandise. What we have here is the *crème de la crème* of the books we sorted out—the most valuable ones. But they have to be in mint condition if we expect to sell them at the InterComiCon."

"We'd *better* unload them," said Bob. "I want my money back! Lucky you read that article about the comics convention in the paper."

Jupiter grinned. "Bob, I'll put you in charge of counting the money afterward. Maybe that will improve your mood."

"We're here," Pete announced. "The Century Grand Plaza."

Bob stared at the glass and steel tower shining against the clear sky. "Pretty ritzy place to sell comics."

"It's August and sweltering," Jupe pointed out. "I'm sure they're happy to get any convention. Shall we park and find the action?"

They drove down a driveway into the hotel's underground parking garage. It looked like a weird concrete forest, with thick round pillars holding up the ceiling—and the building above them. The hotel management had tried to dress up the area with a bright coat of paint. But car exhaust and the shadows cast by all those pillars left the garage looking pretty dingy.

Pete pulled into an empty space. "Last stop. Everybody out."

"We've got a job for some muscles here," Bob said, dragging out the cardboard box of comics.

"Give me a break. I just drove you guys over here!" Pete protested.

"*I* could have driven," Bob said.

"We wouldn't have fit in your VW bug," Pete told him. "Not with Jupe—*and* that box of comic books."

Jupe glared at both of his friends. "*I'll* carry the comics." He grabbed the box. "I've got muscles too, you know. Judo class keeps me in shape."

"You'd be in better shape if you studied karate, like Bob and me," Pete said.

"Not true," puffed Jupe as he headed for the elevator.

The elevator opened as soon as Bob hit the call button.

As the doors closed, however, the guys heard the quick slap of footfalls. Someone was running to catch the elevator. An arm shot through the narrowing space to catch the doors before they shut. The doors sprang open—to reveal a man whose flesh was melting off his body!

2

Let's Make a Deal

THE BOX OF COMICS DROPPED FROM JUPE'S ARMS AS THE horrifying creature leaped into the elevator.

"Hey, sorry." The melting man caught the box in midair. He turned to the Investigators, who shrank away from him. "What's the problem?" he asked, then grinned as he realized the answer. "Oh, my costume!"

He flicked one of the gross-looking folds of flesh dripping off his shoulder. "Latex. I'm dressed as the Outrageous Ooze for the big costume contest. What do you think?"

"V-very realistic," Jupe managed to say.

The elevator reached the lobby, and with a "Got to run!" the Outrageous Ooze disappeared into the crowd. Others in the lobby were dressed as comic-strip characters, too. The Investigators crossed marble tiles and thick carpets to the chrome-framed announcement board. "InterComiCon—main conference hall," Jupe read. "This must be pretty big."

They headed for the conference area and found a line stretching in front of a plain wooden table.

Behind the table sat a girl with dyed blond hair and four-inch dark roots, wearing a black T-shirt with INTERCOMICON STAFF in white letters. "Ten dollars each," she said as the Investigators reached her. She took their money, thumped a stamp on a large black ink pad, and imprinted something on the backs of their right hands.

Jupe noticed that the girl with two-toned hair seemed to hold on to Bob's hand a little longer than necessary. For the first time she smiled.

Pete noticed, too. "If he could bottle whatever makes girls act that way . . ."

Jupe sighed. "I'd buy a case." He studied the stamp mark on his hand. INTERCOMICON—DAY 1. "Cheaper than tickets—smarter too." He glanced at Pete. "We can't go back out and give the stamp to a friend."

They followed Bob to the doorway of the conference hall. But a big guy in another staff T-shirt blocked the way. He checked their stamps, gave them a smile that displayed a chipped tooth, then moved aside. Pete, Bob, and Jupe stepped forward—into sheer craziness.

After the quietly expensive lobby, the scene inside looked like a rug traders' bazaar. The vast open space was broken up by hundreds of folding wooden tables, all arranged in squares to form makeshift stalls. Some tables served as counters, piled high with comics. At the back of each stall rose shelves and display boards, made colorful by comics displayed with their covers out. Carefully wrapped in protective plastic, these comics were obviously serious collector's items.

But even more numerous than the stalls were the people crammed into the aisles between them. Kids and adults pored over stacks of comics, made deals with the people behind the counters, or just tried to push their way through the crowd. Costumed characters showed themselves off. The noise was deafening.

As the three friends stood frozen in the doorway, a tall, thin red-haired man in an InterComiCon T-shirt detached himself from the chaos. He grinned at Jupe, Bob, and Pete.

"First-timers," he said. "I can tell from the stunned look. Welcome to the InterComiCon. I'm Axel Griswold. Supposedly I'm in charge of this madhouse." He glanced at the box in Jupe's arms. "What brings you here, guys?"

After hearing their story, his grin got bigger. "Well, there are lots of dealers," he said, spreading his arms. "But the biggest in the show is a bunch called Kamikaze Komics. They've got the money to give you the best deal. Check 'em out—their stall's over there." He pointed a long, elegant finger at one side of the room.

Following Griswold's instructions, the guys set off into the crowd. Jupe slowed them down for a moment when he stopped at a small stand that sold T-shirts as well as comics. He got each of them a red shirt printed with the message COMIC LOVERS DO IT WITH PICTURES. Working their way deep into the room, the Investigators found the Kamikaze Komics stall. It had a great location—half a wall on the right side, lots of products on sale—and lots of customers. The guys paused before approaching the tables. They wanted to spy out this operation.

Five young guys stood behind the tables, dealing with various customers. One, wearing a single earring, was selling a comic to a young kid. "There you go, *Thunderbeam* Number Three, only four dollars." He held out the comic, whose cover showed a hero blasting a hole through a tank with laser beams from his eyes. "You're lucky, kid. I doubt you'd be able to find this anywhere else in the show."

The kid eagerly handed over his money.

Bob muttered to his friends, "On the way over here I saw that same comic in the one-dollar pile at another dealer's stall."

Pete shook his head. "I remember buying it when it was new—and it only cost fifty cents."

As the Investigators came closer to the Kamikaze stall they saw a TV hooked up to a VCR. A salesman with bleached spiky hair and a black T-shirt was showing a scene from *Astro-Aces*, the hot new sci-fi TV show. "The syndicators send out the new episodes a week in advance. We intercept the satellite beam, tape the show, and you can have it before anybody else in town."

He grinned in triumph as his customer, a guy in his late twenties, eagerly came up with bills.

"He's paying for something he could see for nothing in a few days," Pete whispered.

"And paying for a pirated tape," Bob added.

"I see that 'be the first on your block' is still a strong selling strategy," Jupe murmured, hoisting his box of comics.

A salesman glanced over at them. "Can I help you guys?" The Investigators hesitated. "Hey, if you're not dealing, you're blocking people who will."

"No," Jupe said. "I don't think we're dealing."

As they headed away from the stall he turned to Bob. "Where did you see that other comic? The one without the grotesque price?"

"Back this way," Bob answered. "Near the emergency exit. It was a stall with a crazy name—nutcase or something."

The stall had a madman in its name, not a nutcase—Madman Dan's Comix Emporium. And the man behind the table fit the part perfectly with his wild curly black hair and bushy mustache. "Marty, head upstairs and get some more comic boxes," he said to a young guy, obviously his assistant. Then he turned to a gloomy-looking tall man with a fringe of graying hair around his bald dome. "Back again?"

"Three hundred fifty for that copy of *Fan Fun*," the man offered the dealer.

Madman Dan simply shook his head. "Five."

The man looked gloomier, but tried to bargain. "Four fifty."

"Six."

A note of desperation crept into the buyer's voice. "But the marked price is only four fifty."

"Now it's six," the wild-looking dealer replied.

The man clenched his fists. "All right, six hundred dollars."

Madman Dan's smile got larger. "You waited too long. The price is now seven."

The man's jaw dropped. "Seven hundred! Don't you want anyone to buy it?"

"Close," said Madman Dan. "I don't want *you* to buy it."

The bald man turned on his heel and stormed off. Jupe watched him go. "Do you always treat your customers like that?" he asked.

"Only when they're creeps," Madman Dan replied. "That guy works for one of the major comic publishers. He's also a major creep. Now," he said, looking at the Investigators' box. "Are you here to buy or to deal?"

"We're here to sell," Jupe said, opening the carton.

The dealer checked out the contents. "Some interesting stuff," he said, eyes gleaming. "A couple of Silver Age books in good condition, a lot of fairly recent Number Ones. . . . Tell you what—four hundred for the whole package."

Jupe could feel the color rising in his face. "Only four? That's half what these are worth. I checked out the prices—"

"In the *Overstreet Guide*," Madman Dan finished. "They say you should be getting a lot more, right? But did you read the fine print at the beginning of *Overstreet*? The part where they explain that what they list are averages, and that prices differ from place to place? Not to mention that there's a little thing called profit."

"Profit, not rob—" Jupe said before Bob and Pete managed to pull him out of earshot.

"Don't kill the deal," they warned. "We're making a lot on our twenty bucks."

"We'll make more," Jupe promised them. "It's just a matter of bargaining. . . ."

He turned to face Madman Dan, but his eyes never made it to the dealer. They were snagged by a vision in blue and gold.

It was a tall girl about their age. Glorious blond hair swept nearly to her waist and shone against a blue silky cape. The rest of her outfit looked like a skimpy bathing suit made from glistening gold cloth. It showed off her deeply tanned arms and legs perfectly. As she walked along in her matching gold boots, she was simply breathtaking.

Madman Dan followed Jupe's gaze and grinned. "Eye-catching, huh? She's dressed as Stellara Stargirl for the costume contest. *Her* kind of costume I can understand. So why does someone covered in green slime always win?"

"Um, yes. Now, about these books . . ." But Jupe couldn't take his eyes off the girl.

"Look—" Madman Dan riffled through the box in Jupe's arms and pulled out ten comics. "These titles I can really sell. Can we make a partial deal? Let's say . . . three hundred just for these guys."

Jupe wasn't listening.

"The man made you an offer, Jupe," Bob whispered in his ear.

Jupe tore his gaze back to the comic books. "That begins to sound fairer." His head began turning again, toward the golden girl.

He caught a glimpse, but she disappeared behind a costumed figure all in red. The costume looked like a monk's robe—except for the searing color. As the figure came closer Jupe saw that its face was covered with a black-and-white skull mask.

Jupe shook his head and turned back to Madman Dan. He was all business again. "Right. Three hundred. Those are our most valuable comics, and I suspect you're still doing too well on the deal—"

The costumed character brushed past him, the red robe billowing out. Jupe turned in annoyance.

He saw the figure throw up its arms in a dramatic gesture. Long fingers stretched out, the pale white backs of the hands tightening. Four little balls fell to the floor. Then Madman Dan's whole stall disappeared in smoke!

3

Burned!

THE SUDDEN SMOKE CLOUD CAUSED SOME SHOUTING AND screaming among frightened comic buyers. But that was nothing compared with the screaming that started when the smoke began to clear.

"I've been robbed!" Madman Dan yelled at the top of his lungs. His mop of black curls was wilder than ever, and his mustache bristled. "Where's the guy in the Crimson Phantom costume? I'll kill him!"

Of course, the figure in the red robe had disappeared.

"Pretty slick," Jupe said. "He made his own smoke screen, then vaulted over the table to steal the valuable comics."

He stared at the wooden display board behind the stand, where a big hole had appeared among the comics. Madman Dan was staring, too. "He got my copy of *Fan Fun* Number One . . ."

The same comic that the bald man was bargaining for—and couldn't get, Jupe thought.

". . . And a bunch of twenty- and thirty-dollar

books." The dealer's voice was puzzled, and Jupe soon saw why. Three rows over and two up was a copy of *Flash* Number One—with a price tag of $4,500.

"Maybe the smoke wasn't such a good idea," Jupe suggested. "The thief may have missed what he was really aiming for."

"He did enough damage," Madman Dan said. "Plus on the way across the table he grabbed the books in my hand—*your* comics."

The Investigators stared at one another. The costumed Crimson Phantom had made off with their ten best books—and done them out of at least three hundred bucks!

"Looks like we've got a case to solve," Pete said.

"Case? Solve?" The dealer gave them a sharp look.

"That's what we do," Jupe explained. "Maybe you noticed these were tucked inside our comics." He held out one of their business cards.

"The Three Investigators?" Madman Dan said. "Hey, wait a second." He reached under the table and came out with a small box. Rummaging through, he pulled out a dog-eared card.

"I don't believe it!" said Bob. "He's got one of our old cards."

"Sure," said Madman Dan. "The card with the question marks. It goes for a buck seventy-five."

Jupe blinked. "You mean you're selling this?"

Madman Dan shrugged. "Some people will collect anything." He looked at them for a long moment. "So, you guys solve mysteries. Well, you're just what I need right now. Tell you what. Recover my comics as well as yours, and I'll give you exactly what *Overstreet* says yours are worth."

The Investigators looked at one another. "You've got a deal," Jupe said. He picked up the box of leftover comics and stuck out his free hand.

"Fine. I'm Dan DeMento." The dealer smiled under his shaggy mustache. "With a name like that you can see why people call me Madman."

Jupe grinned. "I'm Jupiter Jones. This is Pete Crenshaw and this is Bob Andrews. I suppose we'll start with the usual question, Mr. DeMento. Is there anyone in particular you suspect?"

"Anyone—or rather everyone." Madman Dan motioned toward the crowd that had gathered around his smoke-bombed stall. Then he spread his arms to take in the whole convention floor. "You've got some of the nuttiest people in California gathered in this room." He grinned. "I'm not saying you have to be crazy to collect comics, but it helps."

"And you're saying they're all suspects?"

DeMento shrugged. "All I can say is, something happens to people when they start to collect things. It doesn't matter *what* they collect. They just aren't quite normal about it."

"You mean they might even steal," Jupe said. "Could the thief sell those books?"

"It wouldn't be easy with something like *Fan Fun*." Madman Dan frowned. "A single book of that value makes dealers nervous. They'd want to know where it came from."

"And the thief couldn't tell them that," Pete said.

DeMento nodded. "Problem is, you're dealing with collectors. The thief may keep the book in his basement for the rest of his life."

As the Investigators chewed over that fact, the bystanders around DeMento's stall were shooed away by hotel staffers, and the regular traffic started again. A twelve-year-old kid walked by with a sheet of thin cardboard covered with panels of black-and-white artwork. "Look what I got," he called to a friend. "A full page of Steve Tresh art from *Crimson Phantom*. Only seventy bucks."

A tall, thin sandy-haired man came forward. His skin was very pale, as if he never went outdoors. "Hey, kid," he said. "I'll give you seventy-five dollars for that."

"No way," the kid replied.

"Okay." The pale man snatched the illustration board with one hand while shoving a fistful of bills at the kid with the other. "That's a hundred bucks," he said. "Enjoy it."

While the kid gaped, the man tore up the illustration and dropped the pieces in an ashtray. Then he pulled out a cigarette lighter and set the pieces on fire.

"Who do you think you are?" the kid yelled. "You have no right to do that!"

A short, fat guy with dark hair and a thick black beard stepped forward. "He has every right. That's Steve Tresh. He wrote and drew those panels."

The kid's jaw dropped. "*You're* Steve Tresh!" he gasped. "Can you sign my convention program?"

Smiling, the pale man scribbled on the kid's program.

"Too bad I couldn't have gotten it on that artwork," the kid said.

The smile disappeared from Steve Tresh's face. "I never autograph Crimson Phantom stuff." He turned away.

The fat guy shook his head at the kid. "You're batting two for two," he said. "Don't you know Tresh got cheated out of that series? Heroic Comics sells all his artwork, and he gets nothing for it. He'd rather burn his art than make it more valuable."

"Steve!" Dan DeMento called to the artist. "I've been wanting to meet you. I had a real collector's item here I wanted you to see." He grimaced. "But it got stolen."

"Hah!" The bearded fat guy walked over to the stall. "A thief complaining about getting robbed. That's rich."

DeMento glared at the man. "Get off my back, Carne."

"You take comics people love and make them pay through the nose for them," Carne accused. "It's people like you who ruin collecting—you and your outrageous prices."

Madman Dan started around the table of his stall, but Steve Tresh grabbed his arm. Jupe could see the convention stamp on the back of the artist's hand as his grip tightened. "Why don't you stay back there," Tresh advised. "Frank here has a point about the business side of comics—and everyone knows that us artists never see any money from all the work you guys sell."

"Gentlemen! Gentlemen!" Axel Griswold hurried over, wringing his slender hands. "I just got news of what happened, DeMento." He shook his head. "Wouldn't you know, this had to happen while I was off the floor. What did the thief get?"

"Nothing much. The best piece was an old fanzine, *Fan Fun* Number One, with some of Steve's work in it." Madman Dan pulled free from Tresh. "I'd hoped to show it to him."

"I know you have differences of opinion about selling comics," Griswold said to DeMento, Tresh, and Carne. "But I'm sure you don't like the idea of thieves in this convention. I hope I can depend on your help."

"Sure. We'll keep our eyes open," Frank Carne promised. "Come on, Steve. It's almost time to catch the beginning of *Rock Asteroid.*" They headed off.

"I've already got some detectives at work on this thing," DeMento said. He introduced the Three Investigators to Griswold.

The red-haired convention boss looked at their card quickly. "Detectives, huh? Well, if there's anything I can do to help, let me know. Right now, though, I've got a new crisis to deal with. We were supposed to start a sixty-hour marathon screening of all four *Rock Asteroid* serials in the Gold Room—but the projectionist didn't show. Frank's going to have a wait."

He sighed. "I got the projector set up, but now I need a volunteer to run it. And the costume contest is about to start too." Griswold rushed off, looking frazzled.

"*Rock Asteroid?*" Bob asked in confusion.

"A science-fiction series from the late forties, I think," Jupe answered. Parking his box of leftover comics with DeMento, he ran after Griswold. Pete and Bob followed. "Can you take a few seconds to help us? Who were those two men just now?"

"The thin, pale guy was Steve Tresh, an artist and writer," Griswold said. "The fat one was Frank Carne. He's a letter hack—writes to the letters pages of all the comics as Frank the Crank." Griswold smiled. "It's a fit name. He has a very big sense of his own importance, telling people the way things ought to be. A troublemaker."

"He seems very friendly with Tresh," Jupe said.

"They've corresponded a lot," Griswold explained. "Until about a month ago, Tresh lived in Ohio. I think he came out here hoping to make it in L.A. But he hasn't done any comics since he arrived."

He sighed. "It made me feel a little sorry for him. I invited him to the convention as guest of honor and even gave him a room. Maybe that was a mistake."

Griswold glanced at his watch. "Sorry, guys, got to go."

The Investigators watched Griswold hurry off.

"What a case," Pete said.

"I think we might have a suspect," Bob suggested.

"Frank Carne? Or Steve Tresh?" Jupe asked.

"I was thinking of Tresh. The theft was outrageous—just like the way he handled that kid with his art," Bob said. "Maybe he didn't like the art in *Fan Fun* either."

"But he turned up right after the comic was stolen," Pete pointed out. "The smoke had barely cleared."

"Well, we know where he's staying," Jupe said. "Why don't we go up to his room and make sure there isn't a smoky comic lying around?"

Jupe got Tresh's room number from the reception desk. Three minutes later the Investigators were standing outside the door of room 318.

Jupe shook his head. "I don't think we can get past this lock," he said. "Not without special equipment."

He turned away, scowling. Then his face brightened

as he noticed that the door to room 320 was ajar. A maid's cart stood outside it.

Two quick knocks and a "Hello?" later, they were inside the empty hotel room.

"What do we do now?" Pete wanted to know. "Bore through the wall?"

"I don't think that will be necessary." Jupe headed to the sliding-glass door and stepped outside onto the balcony. The room overlooked the hotel's central courtyard and swimming pool. But Jupe's eyes went to the left—to the balcony of room 318, about four feet away. "It looks like a short enough jump. We just need someone athletic. A football hero, maybe."

"Oh, no," Pete began. "Not me."

Moments later he was climbing over the steel railing onto the very edge of room 320's balcony. "How do I let you guys talk me into these things?" he muttered. Both of his hands gripped the rail, which bit into the backs of his thighs. As usual, the other guys had stuck him in the jock role—fetch, carry, and now jump.

"Just think of it as a short broad jump," Bob suggested.

"Yeah," Pete grumbled. "Four feet across, but thirty feet down."

He balanced himself on his toes and let go of the railing. Resolutely keeping his eyes on the balcony across from him and off the ground three stories below, Pete jumped.

The other balcony came up. Pete's right foot

landed, but his left foot skidded off the edge. For a heart-stopping second he lurched over, but his hands grabbed the railing. White-knuckled, he pulled himself to safety. He swung over the rail, and when both feet were firmly set on the balcony, he glanced back at his friends. Jupe was pointing impatiently at the sliding-glass door to the room. "Glad to see you were so worried about me," Pete said sourly.

He crossed the balcony and peered through the door. The room looked empty. He tried the door. It slid open without a noise.

Pete stepped inside, scanning the room to make sure Tresh wasn't there. All he saw were piles of illustration board covered with pen-and-ink drawings—artwork Tresh obviously hoped to sell at the convention. Pete flipped through the material, but he didn't see the copy of *Fan Fun*.

He pulled open the door to the closet to see if the red robe was hanging inside. It wasn't. Then Pete turned to search through the dresser. As he pulled open the first drawer he saw movement behind him in the mirror.

Pete whirled—and froze. Leaping from the bathroom was a nightmare figure, a human body with a huge muscular bare chest, tight black jeans, and a fiendishly distorted green lizard's face—the Frog Mutant!

Too late, Pete realized that he was facing a plain, ordinary crook in a monster mask. Before he could even get his hands up, a fist caught him on the cheek.

He staggered back, knocking his head on the framework of the balcony door.

Half-blinded by pain, Pete tried an open-handed chop on his attacker, but he was hurting too much for more than a feeble counterattack. The Frog Mutant blocked it easily. Then he answered with a roundhouse right that sent Pete flying backward, dazed, right out the door.

Pete hit the balcony railing and went tumbling over, with nothing to stop his fall—except the ground below.

4

Astounding Stories

PETE TOPPLED HEADFIRST INTO THE COURTYARD BELOW. Desperately twisting in midair, he managed to take control of his wild tumble. He arched as widely as possible, aiming for the swimming pool. His Olympic-height dive would never have won a medal, but it gave him a safe splashdown.

Pete swam to the surface, gasping and sputtering, still shaken by his narrow escape. At the edge of the pool dozens of arms reached out to him. But Pete stayed where he was, treading water in shock.

Had he landed on another planet? Everyone in front of him looked like an extra from *Star Wars*. He saw robots, green people, characters with a couple of extra heads, and something that looked like a walking furry armchair.

Then he remembered—the costume contest! He'd dropped right into the middle of it. And judging from the dirty looks some of the contestants were giving him, he'd also managed to drench a lot of the people standing at poolside.

Still, some friendly types were on hand to help pull him out—including Jupe and Bob.

"What happened?" Bob asked as he and Jupe steered their dripping friend away from the crowd. "One second you were walking in. Then you came flying out."

"In between I walked into a fist—with plenty of muscle behind it," Pete reported.

"Tresh?" Bob asked. "Or the Crimson Phantom?"

Pete shook his head. "I don't think Tresh was the Phantom. There was no trace of the costume in his room. And the guy who hit me was built like a moose. He had muscles on top of muscles. But I didn't see his face. He was wearing a Frog Mutant mask."

"So we now have a hero stealing comics and a villain breaking into Tresh's room," Jupe said. "I wonder if they're connected."

"We've got company," Bob warned quietly. A man in a hotel blazer—obviously the manager from the insignia on the pocket—came marching toward them. He didn't look friendly. Also running up was Axel Griswold.

"Exactly what happened here?" the manager demanded.

"I—um—fell," Pete said.

"Fell? How? From where?" The manager loomed over Pete, who had dropped into one of the plastic poolside chairs.

"I—" Pete looked around desperately.

"I think you should sue," Jupe cut in. "Those

railings on the balconies are too short and shaky. My friend sneezes, steps back, and goes right over. You're lucky he's an athlete and was able to land safely."

The manager gave Jupe a cold stare. "Are you guests here?" he asked. "What room are you in?"

Axel Griswold stepped forward. "Room 316," he said. "They're with me."

Jupe let Griswold do the talking.

"Ah. I see." The manager turned to the convention chief. "This has not been a pleasant day so far, Mr. Griswold. First the robbery, now this . . . incident. I hope we won't have any more problems." He strode off.

"You and me both," Griswold said. He turned to Jupe. "This had something to do with your investigation, I hope?"

"It did," Jupe assured him. "Pete got jumped while checking something out. Thanks for helping. But if the manager looks for us in room 316 . . ."

"He'll find you. I was going to offer the room to you anyway. It's connected to my suite next door—314. I figured you'd need a place to crash if you were going to stay on the case." Griswold handed Jupe a room key. "Besides, your friend needs a place to dry off—unless that's his costume for Soggyman. Which reminds me." Griswold sighed. "I've got to tell the judges to get this costume show on the road."

He headed for the judges' stand, and the guys went up to room 316. The room contained two double beds, a dresser, and a locked door leading to room

314. Bob and Jupe left Pete wrapped up in towels with his clothes dripping into the bathtub, then headed downstairs again.

The convention hand-stamper was now a pimply-faced guy with a shock of unruly hair. The door guard was the girl with two-toned hair who'd stamped their hands before. She passed Jupe with little more than a glance. But she held on to Bob's hand, smiling up at him.

"Hi, my name's Lori," the girl said.

Bob flashed her his most charming smile. "Lori. That's my favorite name. Lori, did you see a guy in a Crimson Phantom costume leave after those smoke bombs went off?"

Lori gazed into Bob's eyes and shook her head.

Jupe interrupted to ask Lori if she'd seen anyone fitting Frank Carne's description. He wanted to check where Carne had been—and see what the guy could tell them.

Lori scowled at Jupe. "Do you know how many fat guys collect comics?" she snapped. "They range from plump to el grosso. And about nine hundred of them passed here."

"This guy is semifamous," Bob said. "He's a letter hack with a beard . . ."

"Oh, you mean Frank the Crank? Why didn't your friend say so? He came out of here just a couple of minutes ago, heading for the restaurant."

The guys were able to catch up with Carne in the restaurant line. He invited them to join him for lunch. "Let's get an outside table," he said. "Maybe we'll catch more of the show."

Jupe, thinking of another chance to see the blond girl, agreed eagerly.

Bob, thinking of Pete's swan dive, muttered, "I hope not."

They actually got a poolside table. Sitting under its umbrella, they watched the costume contest. As each contestant was announced, he or she would parade around the pool.

Carne ordered two cheeseburgers with the works. Bob contented himself with one. Jupe screwed up his face in pain as he read the menu. "Do you have . . . alfalfa sprouts?" he finally asked the waiter.

"Another diet, Jupe?" Bob tried to hide his smile. His friend had become as famous for his weird methods of trying to lose weight as he was for his detective brain.

"Alfalfa sprouts and a two-mile walk every day," Jupe admitted. "Supposed to melt the pounds off." He looked at the waiter, who shook his head negatively. "No alfalfa sprouts? I'll have a plain green salad—no dressing."

"I don't understand why you kids go around starving yourselves." Carne took a big bite out of his first burger, slurping up the fried onions that hung out over his lips. "Sure you don't want a bite?"

Jupe quickly changed the subject. "What we really need is information about the comics scene. Maybe you could give us some of the low-down."

"Low-down is a good way to describe this business," Carne said, a frown appearing under his heavy beard. "It's set up to rook collectors."

While he talked, an overweight guy in a metal box that looked like a giant toaster waddled around the pool.

Carne sighed. "I got into collecting because I love comics. When I see one with good art or writing, I write in to its letters page. So many people get involved in comics because they love them—then they get ground up by the business end. You saw Steve Tresh burn that art, didn't you?"

Jupe nodded, but his eyes were elsewhere. He'd just spotted the blond girl walking around the pool. Jupe had to pull himself together to listen to Carne.

"Steve's a classic case. Ten years ago, when he was eighteen, Steve invented a hero. Wrote the story, drew it, and got it published in a fanzine—a comic put out by fans. He called his character the Gray Phantom." Carne grinned. "He had to. Most fanzines appear in black and white. So you've got a choice of three colors—black, white, or gray. Anyway, the Gray Phantom was a real sensation, and Steve was discovered. Heroic Comics offered Steve a job, and his hero became—"

"The Crimson Phantom," Bob said. "I used to read that."

"It was a great book. Not just the art, which was fantastic—Steve can really draw. But the stories were wonderful. The Crimson Phantom was a different kind of hero. He didn't run around in long johns. He had those marvelous robes. And then there was the whole secret identity thing."

Bob nodded. "That's right. It really was a secret. *Nobody* knew who the Crimson Phantom was. There were three or four possible characters who might be his secret identity. I remember going crazy looking for clues."

"That book was one of the best comics ever made," Carne said flatly. "Till they ruined it."

"Ruined it?" Jupe asked. "How?"

"Tresh worked with an editor named Leo Rottweiler. He trusted Leo, and Leo got him to sign away his rights to the character. Then Rottweiler totally took over the book, making sure it was 'popular.' " Carne thumped the table. "He started the contest to vote for the secret identity."

Bob looked a little embarrassed. "I remember voting," he said.

"Sure, it was designed to suck in more kid readers. Then he started up two new Crimson Phantom books—*Secrets of the Crimson Phantom* and *The Battling Crimson Phantom*. That meant bringing in new writers and artists. They weren't bad . . . just *ordinary*."

Carne scowled. "Leo killed everything that was special about the character. *The Crimson Phantom* is still around today, selling well. But it's just another comic. Of course, it made Leo Rottweiler the resident genius at Heroic Comics."

"What about Steve Tresh?" Jupe asked as another costumed guy passed their table. He looked like a walking version of Jupe's salad.

"When Tresh saw what they did to his character, he tried to stop it. He couldn't, so he quit. Since then he's had nothing to do with Heroic Comics—or the Crimson Phantom. You saw how he won't even autograph any of his old artwork. Heroic owned it and sold it. Steve would rather burn that stuff than see it sold."

"So you're saying the comic companies cheat comic lovers," Jupe said.

"Kid, *everybody* cheats comic lovers. And we collectors help them." Carne looked around and spotted a dark-haired young man eating at a nearby table. "Hey, Hunter, you have a copy of *Overstreet*?"

The guy put down his burger, dug in his knapsack, and came up with a battered copy of the thick book. "Catch," he yelled, tossing it over.

Frank the Crank caught the book and thumbed through it. "Here it is—*Cerebus*. This is a black-and-white comic, first issue published back in 1977. A mint copy goes for five hundred dollars. But see this under here? A counterfeit copy was made. This mark tells how to recognize it—and says the counterfeits are worth twenty to thirty bucks!"

He shook his head as he handed back the book. "Fans even reward the people who cheat them. They turn counterfeits into collector's items."

Carne frowned again. "And, of course, there are

friendly neighborhood dealers who sell the counterfeits as the real thing."

Jupe looked up. "Like who?"

"I've heard people complain about deals with Dan DeMento," Carne said. "If you're going to deal with Madman Dan, check your watch after you shake his hand."

Just then, the PA system at the pool whined, and the judges announced the winners of the costume contest. First prize went to a guy completely wrapped in fake fur as Slorz the Planet Eater.

At the next table Hunter made a disgusted sound. "What I want to know is why that blond chick didn't win."

Jupe was wondering the same thing as he stared at the girl, but he didn't speak.

Carne got up. "Uh-oh, gotta go. The Muckmen are about to disintegrate Rock's ship."

The Investigators stared as Carne hurried off to pay his bill. Hunter burst out laughing at the looks on their faces. "It's *Rock Asteroid*," he explained. "Frank's seen the movies so often, he only shows up for the good parts."

Rising from the table, Bob muttered, "What a bunch of characters. Is everyone here weird?"

They headed out. From the corner of his eye Jupe caught a flash of gold.

He turned to see the blond girl sitting down at a table near the restaurant entrance. She was with an older woman—probably her mother. As Jupe got nearer he recognized the third person at her table. It was the bald older man who'd tried to buy the copy of *Fan Fun* from Dan DeMento.

Working his way toward the door, Jupe was close enough to overhear the conversation at the table.

The older woman was patting the girl's shoulder as she talked to the bald man. "I think you should go for some photo covers on *Stellara Stargirl*—and here's the perfect model for you, Mr. Rottweiler."

So that's Leo Rottweiler, Jupe thought. I wonder why he's so interested in Steve Tresh's early work.

He turned to join Bob, who was paying the cashier for their lunch. Then a loud, angry voice made him turn again.

Steve Tresh stood red-faced in the restaurant entrance, shouting.

"What's going on around here, Griswold? I just went up to my room—and somebody trashed the place!"

5

Weird People

"STEVE, DO WE HAVE TO TALK ABOUT THIS RIGHT HERE?" Axel Griswold, the convention boss, stood framed in the restaurant doorway looking very embarrassed. A circle of convention-goers gathered, looking extremely interested as Tresh shoved at him.

Jupe and Bob joined the crowd as Steve Tresh started yelling, "Somebody got into my room, tore up my clothes—and slashed all my artwork."

A gasp rose from the conventioneers.

"Why would anyone do a thing like that?" Griswold asked.

"That's what I want to know. Where was your security? What kind of convention is this?"

Griswold tried to calm the artist down. "I can understand how upset you are. If you want to leave . . ."

"Leave?" Tresh's voice rose. "*I* don't want to leave. What I want is that guy—do you know how much of my artwork he ruined? I came here to earn money. And that's what I'm going to do—if I have to make doodles at ten bucks a shot."

He strode away, then turned back. "If you want to find me, I'll be out on the convention floor—*drawing.*"

The crowd broke up, everyone buzzing. Jupe and Bob joined Griswold, who was shaking his head. "See that?" he said. "Even comic-book artists have artistic temperaments."

He shrugged. "Or rent to pay. The main reason Steve agreed to come was the chance of selling his artwork. He must really be hard up if he's willing to stay on after it's been destroyed."

Jupe nodded. Lack of money also made a good motive for theft. "I wanted to ask you about some other people," he said. "Who's that girl in the gold costume?"

Griswold smiled. "Oh, you mean Rainey Fields. She's a cute kid. This is her first major convention. You've got to admit, she makes a perfect Stellara Stargirl." He leaned forward and added confidentially, "Her mother's really pushing for little Rainey to become a star."

"Who's the man at the table?" Jupe asked him.

"That's Leo Rottweiler. He's a senior editor at Heroic Comics. They publish *Stellara Stargirl.* You've got to hand it to Ma Fields. She knows who to go after and how to get them. Don't be surprised if in a couple of months you see Rainey's face smiling at you from some comic rack."

He shook his head. "That woman is a public relations genius. I wish she would work for me."

Griswold reached into his pocket. "If you want to meet them, come to the banquet tonight. I've got some extra tickets. One for you . . ." He handed one to Bob. "One for you . . ." He handed one to Jupe. "And one," he said with a grin, "for your damp friend upstairs.

"It'll be quite a bash," Griswold added. "I expect it to run pretty late. But you guys don't have to worry. You've got a room for the night."

He glanced at his watch. "Got to run. I'm supposed to be introducing the Fan Guest of Honor to the press." He dashed off.

"What's a Fan Guest of Honor?" Bob asked.

Jupe just shook his head. "I don't know why Griswold thinks he needs a PR person. He seems to do a great job all by himself."

Bob grinned. "So what's our next move?"

"Let's go upstairs and get Pete. Then we'll head back home. Pete needs dry clothes, and I suspect we all need something a little better than jeans and T-shirts for this banquet."

Pete's clothes were still slightly soggy, but he pulled them on, uncomplaining, and got his car. As they drove to Rocky Beach Jupe asked, "Who gets your votes for top suspect?"

"Still Steve Tresh," Bob said.

"Why?"

Bob glanced back at Jupe from the front seat. "I can't get the picture of him burning his own artwork out of my head. Looks like he's got something to prove. And we know that his work was in that *Fan Fun* book that got stolen."

"That's a point," Jupe agreed.

"Then there's the fact that he seems to be short of money. He freaked out when his pictures were ruined. But if he needs money, why did he shell out the hundred bucks to pay for the art he burned? He's definitely acting weird."

"Okay, let's say Tresh is our thief," Jupe said. "How does wrecking his room fit in?"

"I'm not sure," Bob said. "But it establishes Tresh as a victim and an unlikely suspect. And now everybody knows there are no stolen comics in the room. Even if Tresh were suspected, the evidence would be gone. I wonder if the Crimson Phantom and the frog guy who jumped Pete were both Tresh?"

"No way," said Pete from behind the wheel. "Tresh is built like a basketball forward. The masked guy in his room had a build like a linebacker."

"Could it have been Frank Carne?" Jupe asked.

Pete frowned. "Nah. I saw this guy's chest. He had muscles. The only muscles Carne has are in his mouth."

"There are other people involved in this Crimson Phantom thing as well—DeMento and Rottweiler." Jupe leaned back in his seat. "Have you noticed how everyone contradicts everybody else? Carne thinks Tresh is a genius. DeMento kind of thinks he's a nut, and Griswold feels sorry for him. DeMento thinks of himself as a businessman; Carne and Tresh think he's a crook."

Bob laughed. "Carne thinks he's a reformer, trying to save comics. Griswold and DeMento think he's a troublemaker." He thought for a second. "How about Rottweiler? I don't think anybody likes him. Tresh must hate him for stealing his hero. Carne thinks he ruined the *Crimson Phantom*. And DeMento certainly gave him a hard time when he tried to buy that fanzine."

"Does it mean something that the book he tried to buy is the one that got stolen?" Pete asked.

"It would make him suspect number two, if I could believe he'd attack you," Jupe told Pete. "But Rottweiler looks like a stork with a potbelly. Not exactly the muscleman you described."

Jupe scowled up at the ceiling of the car. He wanted to add Rainey Fields to the list of suspects. Then he'd have a great excuse to talk to her. But what was she guilty of? Walking past Madman Dan's stall while Jupe was trying to bargain with him?

Of course, it's the oldest trick in the book—send a pretty girl past the scene of a crime to distract all the witnesses, Jupe told himself.

Somehow that didn't make him feel better. In fact, he'd feel pretty miserable if Rainey were involved in the crime.

"This case is weird," Bob finally said.

Jupe nodded. "I guess what Dan DeMento told us about collectors being a little crazy is true," he said.

"And I don't think it helps that what they collect is something as childish as comic books."

"Right," Bob agreed dryly. "If they were smart, they'd collect electronic stuff. Computers are much more mature."

With a spreading grin Bob went on. "Or maybe they ought to collect cars."

Jupe gave his friend a look. "Maybe they should just collect girls, like a certain person I know."

That ended discussion of the case.

When they pulled into Rocky Beach, Pete dropped Jupe off at his house across the street from the junkyard. Jupe caught both his aunt and uncle in and told them he'd be staying overnight at the hotel. Then he spent some time getting a change of clothes together—as well as a jacket and slacks for the banquet.

Within half an hour the other Investigators returned with their overnight bags. Jupe got into Pete's Impala and they headed for the Coast Highway. As they drove back to L.A., Jupe asked Pete to detour through Santa Monica.

"You probably noticed that the sign on Madman Dan's stall said his shop was in Santa Monica," Jupe said. "I looked in the phone book to get the address and saw it wasn't far off our route. I thought we might check the place out—see what kind of operation he's running."

Madman Dan's Comix Emporium was on Pico Boulevard, a simple storefront on the edge of the commercial district. It stood between an unprosperous-looking shop that sold handmade wicker furniture and one that sold vacuum cleaners.

Dan DeMento's store was a blaze of color. The windows were plastered with posters of gaudily-costumed heroes and villains squaring off against each other. Over the door was a poster of Stellara Stargirl soaring high. She really did look like Rainey Fields. Or was it the other way around?

"Well, well," said Pete, pulling up alongside a green van. "Look who's here."

Leaning against the van as two kids staggered out of the store under boxes of comics was Dan DeMento.

"Mr. DeMento!" Jupe called as he got out of the car.

"Oh. You guys." Madman Dan ran a hand through his wild hair, then started riffling through the plastic-wrapped comics he was holding.

"Getting more stock for the convention, I see," Jupe said. "And I guess the comics in your hands will fill in the hole the thief made."

"You deduced right," DeMento said, squaring up the little pile. "I hear one of you guys found a clue about gravity, too. When you fall off a balcony, you wind up in a swimming pool." He shook his head. "Are you guys sure you're detectives?"

Jupe looked down. His glance scanned the cover of the top comic in DeMento's hand. Another copy of *Fan Fun* Number One. What caught Jupe's eye, however, was the price sticker on the bag. Two hundred and fifty dollars.

"I see you're replacing the book that was stolen," he said. "But the price is a lot lower than what you quoted to Leo Rottweiler."

"That was a special book," DeMento began. Then he stopped short. "Why are you questioning me? You should be trying to find that thief."

"We've been investigating," Jupe said. "Talking to people."

"Talking to the *wrong* people, if you ask me," DeMento said. "My friends saw you in the restaurant with Frank the Crank. Don't pay too much attention to that guy. Guys like Frank Carne and Steve Tresh never grow up. I started like them, collecting. But when I made collecting my business, I learned to act like a businessman instead of a kid."

He frowned. "Those guys hold grudges that aren't even sensible. It's the comic dealers and comic shops that keep cult guys like Tresh in business. Does he see that? No. He and Carne just love to see guys like me suffer."

Jupe nodded. The question was, would they go as far as theft to *make* DeMento suffer?

6

Arts—and Craftiness

THE INVESTIGATORS LEFT DEMENTO AT HIS STORE AND drove to the Century Grand. Pete sighed from behind the wheel. "I guess I didn't help us very much when I took that fall," he said. "Looks like DeMento thinks of us as the Three Stooges instead of the Three Investigators."

"We'll just have to make him forget that." Jupe sat up in his seat. "And the way to do it is some heavy-duty legwork. We've got to find out who was where when those comics were stolen."

"We know where DeMento was," Bob said. "He was standing in front of us."

And we know where Rainey Fields was—heading away from us as the Crimson Phantom approached. Maybe I should ask her . . . Jupe pushed that thought to the back of his mind as he went over the other possible suspects. "I'd like to know where Leo Rottweiler was. And Frank the Crank. Most especially, where was Steve Tresh when the crime went down? *That* might tell us something."

They parked in the underground garage, took the elevator to their room, and dropped off their stuff. Then they headed for the main conference room. Jupe thought the crowd outside the convention doors had thinned a little. But the madhouse inside seemed even more jam-packed than before. The husky security guard with the chipped tooth was back in position. He blocked their way and checked the stamp marks on their hands.

Jupe led his pals through the crowd toward the far end of the room. The mob scene grew denser as they came to a row of tables. Behind the tables sat artists, sketching and signing autographs. Some of the tables had posters set up on them, as well as books, comics, magazines, and piles and piles of illustration board with comic panels.

The artists seemed to be doing a landslide business. Hundreds of people were lined up in front of them, from kids clutching old comics to middle-aged men with fat wallets coming to buy artwork. Most of the fans were shiny-eyed at the chance to meet their artist-heroes. But some were out of hand, pawing through the artwork for things to buy and demanding autographs on everything from T-shirts to cardboard coffee cups.

In between autograph requests the conversations were equally outrageous. "*Slime Man* just hasn't been the same without you, Jack," a fevered fan told one artist. "Nobody draws slime like you do."

Another young fan came up to an artist and yelled,

"You ruined *Robot Avenger*. Stebbins knew how to draw robots. You made the robot's head look like a Volvo. They ought to can you from that book. Oh, and by the way, can you sign these pages for me?"

The artist stared at the kid. "If you don't like my work, why are you collecting it?"

"I can get twice what I paid for this with your autograph on it," the kid said without batting an eye.

Shaking his head, the artist signed.

Jupe couldn't believe it. "I guess it's one way to ditch a fan," he said. "Let's find Steve Tresh."

Tresh was engulfed by the longest line of all. The pasty-faced artist sat at a bare table, quickly dashing off sketches of various heroes and villains. Some of his fans had come by to sympathize at the way his artwork had been destroyed. They were happy to buy new sketches.

Some of the younger kids were demanding that Tresh draw Crimson Phantom sketches or autograph Crimson Phantom comic books for them. "C'mon!" one teenager yelled, waving a comic in the artist's face. "What else are ya famous for? Sign this!"

Tresh grabbed the kid's wrist. "I've worked on twenty other characters besides the Crimson Phantom—other people's and my own. If you want a signature for that comic, get Leo Rottweiler's. It's his book now."

"Everybody autographs things," the loudmouth insisted. "You gotta."

"No, I don't." Tresh shook his head. "And if you

keep shoving that book in my face, I might 'accidentally' spill a bottle of ink all over it."

The teenager still waved the book.

"It might even accidentally get torn in two."

The pushy fan snatched the book back and disappeared into the crowd.

"Let me take a crack at Tresh," Bob whispered to the other Investigators. He wormed his way through the crush. Lots of heads turned to give him dirty looks, but he kept moving. How would he get Tresh's attention? Finally he decided on the direct approach.

"Mr. Tresh!"

Steve Tresh glanced up. "What now?" He looked at Bob's empty hands. "At least you don't have anything idiotic for me to sign, so I guess you want a sketch. Who can I do for you? I'd say you were a Killer Brain fan. Am I right?" His pen was already dashing over the paper.

"Speaking of killers, I saw you in action right after Dan DeMento's stall got ripped off. That was an incredible move, snatching the art from that kid."

Tresh's pen skidded to a stop.

"Too bad you weren't around when the comics were snatched," Bob went on. "You might have caught the guy who grabbed them. Where were you right then? Did you see him?"

Tresh stared at Bob in silence. The artist's fans started getting annoyed. "Hey, chump!" one called out. "You want to talk to the man, wait your turn like everybody else."

"C'mon, Steve," another yelled. "We've got business to do. Get rid of this guy."

"Where was I?" Tresh finally said to Bob. "In the middle of this zoo, right here." His voice turned sour as his pen started scribbling again. "At least then I had artwork to sell. Get lost, will you? I'm busy right now."

He held up his sketch. "Anybody want to buy a Killer Brain?"

Bob stared, taken aback by the quick way he'd been dismissed. But then, he realized, Tresh had lots of practice with this unruly crew. Dozens of voices were shouting in his ears, bidding for the picture. Bob just managed to lean over and flip a business card to Tresh. "Maybe we can talk again," he said. Then he started to squash his way out of the mob.

Jupe and Pete were waiting on the fringes of the crowd right where Bob had left them.

"What did he say?" Pete asked.

"Tresh said he was right there," Bob said, glancing back at the crowd. "If the same mob was around, he'd have a lot of witnesses." Bob tried to pull his polo shirt straight, but for once his tidy image was completely shot.

"Nice claim." Jupe's eyes narrowed. "But then how did he turn up at DeMento's stall so soon after the robbery?"

"He and Frank Carne showed up at the same time," Bob said. "Maybe they were together."

Jupe nodded. "Good point. Now, where do we find Carne?"

A familiar face suddenly appeared in the crowd—Hunter, the dealer who had lent Carne his copy of *Overstreet*. "Hey, guys," he said. "What's happening?"

But when he heard their question, he shook his head. "I haven't seen Frank the Crank for an hour." He suddenly grinned. "You could try staking out the Gold Room. Head out the front, hang a left, another left, and go all the way down the hallway. Sooner or later Frank will turn up for one of the good parts of *Rock Asteroid*."

"Thanks," Jupe said. "and how about Leo Rottweiler? Have you seen him?"

"Sure," Hunter said, pointing. "He's over there with a bunch of Heroic people—some kind of PR stunt for their new Heroic Classics series."

Jupe followed Hunter's arm to catch the flash of cameras— and the glint of a gold costume. He quickly led the way to a cleared area where a group of Heroic Comics artists were posing beside life-size cardboard cutouts of their characters.

But the cameras and TV lights were all clustered around the cutout of Stellara Stargirl. The reason didn't take much detection. Standing next to it was Rainey Fields, still in costume, giving a dazzling smile to the news people.

Her mother stood on the sidelines talking sweetly to all the reporters nearby. And behind her, looking torn between delight over the news coverage and annoyance at being upstaged, was Leo Rottweiler.

Jupe stepped up to the editor. "Mr. Rottweiler, could I ask you a question?"

"Why not, kid?" Rottweiler ran a hand over his bald head. "Nobody else seems to be."

"I noticed you were at Dan DeMento's stall shortly before the theft," Jupe said. "Do you think the comic you were looking at was worth stealing?"

Rottweiler stared at him. "What kind of question is that? And where do you get off asking it?"

"My friends and I are investigating the case for Mr. DeMento." Jupe handed Rottweiler a business card. "I wanted your expert opinion . . ."

"You want more than that." Rottweiler flicked a finger against the card and glared at Jupe. "I wasn't even on the convention floor, much less near that stall when it was robbed. Some idiot fan trapped me in an argument outside the Gold Room."

"A fan?" Jupe asked.

"Frank Carne." Rottweiler frowned, as if even the memory annoyed him. "He came out of the Gold Room, where they were showing that stupid movie. I guess there'd been some sort of foul-up with the projector. Axel Griswold was in there trying to fix it. Carne came out to bother me with his nonsense."

"And then?"

"Somebody came by and told us about the commotion at DeMento's stall. Carne went back to take a look at it. I figured Griswold should know about it, so I got him. Frankly, I was happy to get away from Carne. He has a very big opinion of himself." Rottweiler smiled nastily. "Almost as big as his waistline."

The editor turned away. "Now, if you'll excuse me, I have business—answering *legitimate* questions."

Jupe stared at the man as he walked off. It seemed to him he was seeing more backs in this case than anything else.

A hand landed on Jupe's shoulder and he turned to find Axel Griswold standing beside him.

"I saw you talking with Leo Rottweiler," the convention boss said. "Is he involved in your case?"

"Maybe," Jupe said. "He was at DeMento's stall right before the robbery. But he has an alibi for the actual robbery itself—which we'll have to check out."

"Who else have you been checking?"

"We want to find Frank Carne—and we've already spoken to Steve Tresh," Jupe said.

Griswold's eyes glowed with interest. "Does Steve have an alibi too?"

"He said he was over in the artists' section selling stuff. I suppose about nine hundred autograph seekers will back him up."

"I don't think so." Griswold was frowning. "Right before I met you guys at the entrance, I passed by the artists' area. I know for sure there was no crowd at Steve's table—because Steve Tresh wasn't there."

7

Dinner and a Show

"LET'S NAIL DOWN THOSE ALIBIS TONIGHT," JUPE SAID TO his friends as they stepped into the banquet room. "And I'd like to talk to some people who were around DeMento's stall at the time of the robbery." He nervously straightened his tie.

Pete's eyebrows went up. "*Some* people?" he said with a grin. "Like maybe that blonde who made your eyes pop out? I never saw such a struggle. Jupiter Jones making a money deal and being distracted by true love."

"Knock it off." Jupe's voice got gruff, and he could feel his cheeks turning red. But he hoped that Rainey Fields would be around.

She was, in another Stellara Stargirl outfit. This one was more formal, with a high-necked cape. Rainey's blond hair was done up in a fantastic head-dress, and she'd added a skirt made from strips of gold silk to the basic outfit. Whenever she moved, it showed off her fantastic long legs. If anything, she turned even more heads in this costume than she had all day.

Jupe waited until Rainey's mother was deep in conversation with some comic-book biggie before he came over to talk.

"Hey, you're one of the guys tracking down the stolen comic books," Rainey said after Jupe introduced himself. Her big hazel eyes sparkled with interest. "Everyone on the convention floor has been talking about you—especially since your friend fell in the swimming pool."

"Ah—yes," Jupe replied. Great, he thought to himself. You're supposed to be questioning her and all you can come up with is "Ah—yes." Pull yourself together!

"At the approximate time of the robbery you were in the vicinity of the robbery site," Jupe found himself saying. This is worse, he thought. I sound just the way I did back when I was ten, trying to impress the grownups.

Rainey looked at him oddly.

"Dan DeMento's stall," Jupe went on, his collar suddenly feeling two sizes too small. "I personally observed—ah, I saw you there."

Rainey grinned. "I guess a lot of people were observing me. This getup is pretty hard to miss." She pulled the cape around herself. "I don't know where I got the nerve to enter the contest."

"You look admirable—um, fine," Jupe said.

"Do you always talk that way?" Rainey gave him a sideways look. "With instant translations?"

Only when I'm tripping over my tongue, Jupe

thought. But he managed to say, "It's the first time I ever interviewed a superbeing."

Rainey's grin turned to a full-out smile. "I didn't see the perpetrator—isn't that what they always call him?"

"But maybe you saw something—anything out of the ordinary."

Rainey shrugged. "I didn't really notice a thing. To tell the truth, I was fighting a bad case of stage fright. You see, this is my first big convention."

Tiny lines appeared on her forehead as she thought. "Wait. I remember Madman Dan's stall, because of that crazy name. There was a guy with frizzy black hair behind the table"—she glanced at Jupe—"and *you* were talking to him!" She concentrated some more. "There was a tall guy standing beside you—and a real cute blond guy."

Jupe sighed. Trust any girl to remember Bob.

"Did you notice anything else?"

Rainey shook her head. "Not really. I was on my way to that costume contest, and that's all I was thinking about. Oh. That guy in the Crimson Phantom costume breezed past me. He was going pretty fast—his robes billowed out. At least it wasn't Slime Man. Could you imagine him brushing past you?" She wrinkled her nose.

"Did you notice anything in particular about him?" Jupe asked.

"What was there to notice? He was a guy dressed as the Crimson Phantom—in a big hurry."

"Think for a minute," Jupe said. "Picture him in your mind. Tell me what he's doing."

Rainey closed her eyes. "He's reaching inside his costume—getting something out."

"He was probably pulling out the smoke bombs he dropped in front of the stand." Jupe looked at her closely. "Did you see what he was wearing under his costume?"

Frowning, Rainey shook her head. "Sorry. I really wasn't paying attention. I was too busy worrying about that dumb contest."

"When the bombs went off, there was a lot of yelling and screaming. Did you notice that?"

"Sure," said Rainey. "I looked back for a second. But I had to get to the contest, so I kept going. I was afraid I'd be late. Oh, and I saw the guy in the Crimson Phantom costume running."

Jupe leaned forward. "He brushed past you again?"

"No. I just caught a glimpse of red, heading away from me, like toward the exit."

"Where were you going?"

"You know where all the artists are sitting?" Rainey said. "At the far end of the room from the entrance? That's where they got us together for the contest."

"You're sure he was heading for the doors?"

Rainey shrugged. "There's no way I can be sure. I saw smoke, and a flash of red over somebody's shoulder—as if the robe was flapping. After that, I didn't see the guy again."

"Nobody at the entrance saw him," Jupe said.

"You'd think a man in a red robe would be hard to miss." He looked at Rainey, trying to think of something else to say. But nothing came into his head. "I guess those are all my questions."

"Can I take a turn now?" Rainey said with a grin.

"Oh—sure," Jupe said. She wants to talk, he thought to himself. This is a good sign.

"Your cute friend—does he like blondes?"

For a long second Jupe stared at Rainey. Then he heard a voice saying, "Oh, Rainey, dear."

"I think I hear your mother calling," Jupe said quickly. He handed Rainey one of the Investigators' business cards. "Maybe we'll talk again. Keep this—um—if your costume has pockets."

Rainey laughed. "I'll find someplace to tuck it away."

They let themselves be separated by the mingling crowd. A few minutes later Bob grabbed Jupe's arm. "I found Frank Carne."

Jupe grinned. He knew Bob would handle that job. "What does he say?"

"The same thing as Rottweiler. They were outside the Gold Room arguing."

"Over what?" Jupe wanted to know.

"Are you ready for this? Over the artwork in the latest *Crimson Phantom* books. Rottweiler brought in a new artist. Carne says this new guy stinks—he can't do shadows."

"Shadows?"

"When Tresh created the Crimson Phantom, he

used all sorts of spooky highlighting—especially the black shadows on the character's skull mask," Bob explained. "The new artist took them all out. Carne says he turned the Crimson Phantom from a menace into a wimpy coloring book character."

"Interesting," Jupe said. "Remember the mask on the thief? It had black shadows painted on. I guess Carne would approve."

"Approve?" Bob asked.

"For the moment, let's just say it's the kind of mask a purist would wear," Jupe suggested. "And here's another thing to remember. Billowing robes are a great disguise. You can't tell the shape of the guy under them." He patted his own ample stomach. "Now let's find Pete and get some seats."

"Seats are taken care of," Bob said. "Carne invited us to eat at his table."

"Okay, so where's Pete?" Jupe started scanning the crowd, when a bustle of movement caught his attention. Leo Rottweiler had just put a hand on Steve Tresh's chest. "You've got a smart mouth, Tresh. I've heard some of the remarks you've made about me."

"You don't like me calling you a crook?" the hot-tempered artist shot back. "Wait till you hear my speech!"

"That does it!" Rottweiler shoved Tresh backward and went to throw a punch. Tresh staggered into the crowd but came back, fists ready. The two men were actually swinging at each other when someone pushed between them.

It was the beefy security guy from the convention door, with a jacket over his black T-shirt. He grabbed Tresh and swung him away. Rottweiler landed a glancing blow to Tresh's cheek before Axel Griswold appeared and grabbed the editor's arm.

"Brave, Rottweiler, real brave," Tresh sneered. The convention staffers led the two men up on the dais, seating them at opposite ends. Taking that as a hint, the crowd members began finding their own seats.

Bob and Jupe found Pete and headed for Carne's table. Jupe looked back at the glowering artist. "What did you find out about Tresh, Pete?"

"Nobody saw him around the artists' tables at the time of the robbery," Pete reported.

"It was very confused around there, from what I hear," Jupe said. "That's where the people were assembling for the costume contest."

Pete shrugged. "I talked to a bunch of artists. They say he wasn't there."

"I'd say we have some more questions for Mr. Tresh," Bob said.

"Let's eat first," said Jupe. Then he looked forlornly at the wilted salad on the table. "Anyone want to trade their salad for the rest of my meal?"

Frank Carne, already at the table, was only too happy to oblige. Actually, Jupe made out well on the deal. The salad wasn't bad compared with dinner—rubber chicken with burned potatoes.

"Guess we can't complain," Bob whispered to Pete. "We got in for free."

They couldn't follow their after-dinner plan of questioning Tresh, either. As it turned out, he was the after-dinner speaker.

"I'd like to thank Axel Griswold for asking me to give you a few words," Tresh said with a smile. "It's the first time since I moved to California that anyone has paid for my words."

The audience gave him a mild laugh.

"I know some people think I've given up comics entirely since I came out here." Tresh shook his head. "They don't have to worry. I've been working on a new comics hero, and you'll be seeing him very soon."

Happy applause greeted this announcement.

"Who are you doing it for?" someone called out.

Tresh turned in the direction of the voice. "I'm not doing it 'for' anybody but myself. This time I'm publishing independently. Less corporate hassles that way. And"—his eyes flashed to Leo Rottweiler on the far end of the dais—"less chance of theft."

The editor's bald head was a dull shade of red as he glared at Tresh.

Steve Tresh went on to discuss the problems of self-publishing. When he finished, he was mobbed by an enormous crowd of eager fans.

At the Investigators' table, Frank Carne nodded approvingly. "I'd heard rumors that Steve was working on something," he said. "Glad to see it's for real." He combed his fingers through his beard thoughtfully. "I wonder where he's getting the money, though."

"I thought that's why he was here," Jupe said. "To make money."

"He'd need more than he'd make at a convention to finance a book of his own," Carne objected. "Independent publishing takes big bucks."

"Another question for Steve Tresh," Bob murmured.

Jupe nodded. Tresh had no alibi for the time of the crime. And now it seemed as if he had a motive—money.

Glancing over at Pete, Jupe caught his friend stifling a yawn. "I know how you feel," Jupe said. "What do you say we hold off on talking to Tresh and head up to room 316? I could use some sleep."

"Us, too," Bob and Pete agreed.

"Well, good night, guys," Frank the Crank said. "I'll be leaving pretty soon myself. It's coming up to where Rock zaps the Muckmen army with the blutellium bomb."

Shaking their heads, the Investigators left.

On their way out they passed the table where Rainey Fields sat. As usual, her mother was deep in conversation with somebody. Rainey looked over and smiled.

Was that smile for me? Jupe wondered. Or for Bob?

The thought continued to bother him even after he'd gotten into bed. From the regular breathing around him, he could tell his two friends were already asleep. But he lay in the darkened hotel room with Rainey's smiling face still appearing before his eyes.

She was friendly enough. Maybe, just maybe—He shook his head. Maybe I'm getting out of my league here. . . .

His thoughts were interrupted by a tiny rattle at the door to the room. Jupe sat up in bed. Somebody was trying to break in!

8

Attack of the Killer Cyclops

THE DOOR OPENED.

Jupe caught a glimpse of the intruder, a fuzzy figure silhouetted in the doorway. The door automatically swung shut behind him. The intruder was in the room.

Jupe's hand shot to the lamp on the bedside table. But in the dark and unfamiliar room, he misjudged the distance. The lamp fell over with a crash.

"Hey! What—" Both Bob and Pete were surprised to be awakened from a sound sleep. But when they realized there was an intruder, they jumped at him.

It was a confused battle in the darkness. Jupe took a swing, but found himself pulling his punch. What if I hit one of the guys by mistake? he thought.

The intruder had no such problem—anyone he hit was an enemy, so he hit hard.

As Jupe groped his way forward the unseen enemy lashed out, kicking Jupe in the stomach. Jupe gasped in pain and sat down hard. But he used his judo training to turn the drop into a controlled fall. Jupe rolled to his left, slapping the floor, and heaved himself upright. He headed for the wall. If he could just find the light switch . . .

He heard a grunt, then a sharp cry from Bob. "He's getting away!" More sounds of confused movement cut the darkness—and then Jupe's fingers found the switch!

The ceiling fixture came on, dazzling the Investigators—just as the intruder threw open the door and made a run for it.

"Come on!" The three tumbled through the door and headed down the hallway. Their quarry had already made it to the first bend. They rounded the turn, then stumbled to a surprised halt.

A long hallway stretched before them—longer than the intruder could have run. Yet nobody was there.

"Must have ducked into one of the rooms," Bob gasped. He had a hand to his side—he'd been kicked, too.

"Yeah. Or—" Pete ran to a small alcove in the hall, decorated with an EXIT sign. He threw the door open and heard the pounding sounds of fast movement. "He's taking the fire stairs! Let's go!"

Jupe could feel the metal stairs shaking as they thundered down. The guy ahead couldn't help but know they were still on his trail. Jupe just wanted to catch up with this guy. For their stolen comics, and for that foot in the gut. He could feel his hands turning into fists as he pushed himself to keep up with his friends.

The stairs ended at the entrance to the hotel's underground garage.

Together the guys rammed into the panic bar on the door, throwing it open to reveal one of the darker corners of the complex. Heavy pillars blocked out most of the nearby light, and the ceiling fixture over the door had a broken bulb.

Pete dashed forward, eager to have it out with the intruder. He turned left on the concrete floor, yelling, "This way!"

Legs pumping, he outdistanced his friends, rapidly gaining on the dark figure. "He's mine!" he shouted to the others. "For punch . . . on . . . balcony!"

Pete took a final giant step, then hurled himself forward in a tackle. It should have brought down the intruder.

Instead, the shadowy figure turned and caught Pete in midair with a backhand slam. Pete bounced into one of the concrete pillars, then disappeared behind it.

"Pete!" Bob skidded to a halt and knelt beside his friend. "Are you all right?"

"Knocked the breath out of me," Pete gasped, pushing himself up. "Come on!"

Bringing up the rear, Jupe had seen Bob stop for Pete. Now he was the advance guard as he rounded the pillar. He ran about five more steps, when he was blinded by the high beams of a car's headlights.

Make that *headlight*. The car in front of him was a Cyclops—only one light worked. And judging from the size of it, it was probably a van.

But if the van's lights didn't both work, its engine was fine. It roared to life as the driver gunned the gas, sending the vehicle leaping straight at Jupe!

He barely had time to shout a warning as he flung himself aside. Bob and Pete, just rounding the pillar, spilled to the ground as the van screeched past them.

Jupe leaped to his feet and raced after the van. But it was already squealing up the exit ramp and making a quick right turn. By the time Jupe reached the top of the ramp the van had disappeared in traffic. His shoulders slumped as the others joined him. "Anybody get the license plate?" he asked.

"License plate! Are you kidding?" Pete said.

"If I'd stood still, I might have it printed on me now," Bob added.

"I didn't get the number either," Jupe admitted. "Or a look at the driver. Did we notice *anything*?"

"The van was a dark color. Gray, I think," said Bob.

"Black," Pete insisted.

Jupe shook his head. "I thought more like dark green."

"And one headlight was out," Pete said.

"Right. So we've got a dark Cyclops van. There should be only a few thousand like it in Los Angeles." Jupe sighed. "No problem at all."

"We've got a more immediate problem," Bob announced.

Pete and Jupe braced themselves. "What now?"

"Did either of you guys bring the key to our room?

When the door shut behind us, it automatically locked."

Jupe looked down at his pajamas, then at his friends' sleeping gear. Pete was in running shorts, Bob in drawstring sweatpants. "You mean we'll have to go to the registration desk and ask for a key—dressed like this? If word of this gets out, everyone will be *sure* we're the Three Stooges."

He stepped onto the sidewalk and made a left toward the front of the building. "Come on. We might as well enjoy a walk in the evening air. Besides, the front door is closer to the reception desk."

The wall rising beside them was solid concrete, but it soon turned into glass panels that dipped in, making room for a little garden and a side entrance to the hotel.

"Maybe we can sneak in through here," Pete suggested, stepping past a royal palm.

In the shadows under the tree something moved and groaned. The Investigators realized it was a human figure pulling itself up, a figure with a thin, angry face—Steve Tresh!

"What happened to *you*?" Jupe gasped.

Tresh had a swollen lip, bruises, and a definite mouse growing under one eye. He started to frown, then winced at the pain in his lip.

"I don't know what happened. I got tired of the noise in there and stepped outside. Next thing I know, somebody's jumping me." Tresh stood up, moving very slowly and carefully. "He worked me over pretty well. I never got a good look at the guy's face. But I have an idea who did this."

"Who?" Bob asked.

"Who was the last guy to take a swing at me?" Tresh asked, heading for the hotel entrance. "Leo Rottweiler."

Tresh went through the door, with the Investigators right behind. The artist was too upset to notice the guys' sleeping gear. Bob turned toward the reception desk, but Jupe shook his head. "Forget the keys."

Instead they followed Tresh across the lobby, their eyes straight ahead, trying to ignore the pointing and laughing. Jupe could see the red rising in Pete's ears. At least the elevator was right there. They stepped aboard and Tresh pressed three.

"Most of the pros and convention celebs are on the lower floors," Tresh explained as the elevator headed up. "I happened to hear that Rottweiler has room 335. We're going to pay him a little visit."

He marched down the hallway with the guys trailing after him and began pounding on the door to room 335. Leo Rottweiler answered it. His tie was loosened, but he was still in his suit.

Tresh grabbed him by the throat and started shaking him. "You didn't think you were going to get away with this, did you?" he yelled.

"Tresh, what are you doing?" cried Rottweiler. Confused voices came from inside the room as the Investigators tried to disentangle Tresh from the paunchy editor. They looked up to see Axel Griswold rushing toward them. Behind him were a bunch of comics people with glasses in their hands.

"What am I doing?" Tresh asked, lunging at Rottweiler again. "I'm going to rearrange your face, the way you tried to do mine."

"Why—why—what are you talking about?" Rottweiler stammered.

"Don't play innocent," Tresh shouted at him. "You jumped me outside."

"When did this happen?" Griswold wanted to know.

"It was only a few minutes ago. Ask him!"

But Griswold was shaking his head.

"No way," he said. "The party came up here to Leo's room a while ago. He couldn't have left—he's the host."

"Difficult, but not impossible," Jupe said.

"Maybe," Griswold said. "But I can personally vouch for the last half hour." He pointed at a large couch in the middle of the suite. "Leo and I were sitting over there talking."

He looked at Jupe right in the eyes. "And I think I'd have noticed if he left to beat Steve up."

9

Different Strokes

THE NEXT MORNING JUPE AWOKE EARLY. FROM THE SOUNDS of regular breathing around him, he realized Bob and Pete were still sleeping. He slipped out of bed carefully, without waking them. He dug a pair of swimming trunks out of his bag and put them on with a baggy shirt. Then he tiptoed toward the door—after making sure he had the key.

Jupe had decided that the pool would be the best place to do some thinking about the case. While he floated in the water, he could let his mind drift through all the facts and opinions they'd collected. Each time they made a step forward, the case became more confusing.

For instance, meeting Steve Tresh up close had changed the artist's "angry man" image. Yes, he had been angry, but he'd also shown a sense of humor. Jupe found it hard to imagine him as a thief.

Not only that, it was impossible for Tresh to have been the midnight visitor who broke into the Investigators' room. The guys had all agreed last night that the fight in the darkness could never have done that much damage to Tresh. They just hadn't been swinging hard enough to make him look like a human punching bag. So where had Tresh gotten those bruises?

Could he have beaten himself up to divert suspicion? That didn't make sense. Tresh wouldn't have had enough time between the disappearance of the van and his discovery by the Investigators.

For a second Jupe smiled at the ridiculous picture of Tresh ramming his head against the windshield to simulate injuries while deciding where to ditch the van. *That* theory wouldn't work. And somehow he didn't see Tresh as somebody who'd play for the sympathy vote.

Okay. So who beat up Tresh, and why? Did the beating tie in with the theft of the comics? Tresh was still the main robbery suspect. But the beating said somebody else was involved. It looked like they were stuck with a whole new mystery.

Jupe took the elevator downstairs. As he cut through the lobby on his way to the pool, he heard his name being called. He turned to see Axel Griswold hustling over to him.

"You're up early," the convention boss said.

"So are you," Jupe replied. "Especially after that late-night party."

"I don't have a choice," Griswold responded with a smile. "The earlier you start to work on conventions, the more disasters you get to find. Besides, I should count myself lucky. I managed to get *some* rest. There are red-eyed guys in the Gold Room who've spent the last twenty hours watching *Rock Asteroid*. When you come to a convention, you kiss sleep good-bye."

Actually, Griswold didn't seem to have missed much sleep. He was wearing fresh jeans and a new InterComiCon T-shirt. With his clipboard under his arm, he looked bright-eyed and ready for anything.

Jupe was sure he himself looked tired and grumpy, if not downright surly.

"How are you coming along with your case?" Griswold asked.

"We're still digging, and we keep coming up with puzzling things. I suppose you've guessed that Steve Tresh is a pretty strong suspect, especially since you knocked a hole in his alibi. But if he's the thief, why did somebody trash his room? And why was he beaten up?"

Griswold nodded, looking interested. "And what answers have you come up with?"

"None, so far. But all of a sudden someone seems determined to make Tresh's life miserable. That started me wondering if we haven't gotten things mixed around somewhere. Certainly Tresh comes off looking more like a victim than a crook."

As usual, Griswold glanced at his watch. "Thanks for sharing your thoughts with me," he said, heading off. Then he turned back, an expression of concern on his face. "You realize, though, there is another explanation for what's been happening to Tresh."

"What's that?" asked Jupe.

"The old-fashioned phrase is 'a falling-out among thieves.' "

◆ ◆ ◆

Chewing over those last words, Jupe was not in a good mood when he reached the pool. He dove in and started doing laps back and forth.

Exercise was never Jupe's thing. But he did enjoy swimming, with his powerful legs churning up the water and sliding him along. He swam the way he solved cases—slowly and methodically.

He broke into a powerful crawl, leaving his body on autopilot as he tried to fit the pieces of the case together. Somebody had attacked Steve Tresh. Someone had also attacked Pete in Tresh's room. And then there was the someone who had punched out all the Investigators last night. Not to mention the someone in the Crimson Phantom costume who stole the comics. Did all those someones add up to the same person?

Pete hadn't gotten a look at his attacker's face because of the frog mask, but he had seen a lot of muscle. That didn't match the looks of any of the theft suspects. Tresh was tall and lean, Carne was fat, Rottweiler had a potbelly—and Rainey Fields didn't fit the description at all.

So either the thief was somebody they didn't know about, or there was more than one person involved. As Jupe started examining possible combinations, he heard a splash behind him. He turned to get a blurry glimpse of a girl in a red tank suit coming up from a dive. Short brown hair was plastered around the sides of her face as she started swimming on a course parallel to his. Jupe continued on his way—*stroke-kick, stroke-kick.*

The girl in red soon caught up with him, then passed. By the time Jupe reached the far end of the pool, she was already on her return—the backstroke this time instead of the crawl.

As Jupe swam, he sneaked a peek over at the girl. She was pretty, tanned, and obviously enjoying herself. He'd barely reached the middle of the pool before she was coming back at him again.

Jupe stolidly kept up the same pace as the girl kept zipping back and forth. He felt like an old barge laboring its way along while some sleek hydrofoil sliced through the water past him. But Jupe knew better than to try to make a race of it. This kid definitely had him outclassed.

He outlasted her, though. After maybe twenty laps (to about a dozen of Jupe's) the girl swam to the side of the pool. Jupe found himself watching as she pulled herself out of the water, brushing back her hair with a quick gesture. Definitely gorgeous. And young. A teenager.

Treading water in the middle of the pool, Jupe watched her go over to one of the lounge chairs and pick up a towel. A beach bag lay under the chair. Obviously she'd staked her claim before she dove in.

After a quick rubdown with the towel, the girl lay

back in the chair. Then she got up and turned the chair toward the sun.

The slight adjustment knocked one of the legs of the lounge chair against her bag. It fell on its side and spilled open. The girl never noticed as she plopped back in the chair.

Jupe noticed, however. He stared at the bag—or rather, what was now spilling out of it.

Comic books.

Jupe was so surprised that he stopped moving for a second, and sank beneath the water.

Then he got his arms and legs in gear again and headed straight for the edge of the pool.

Even from the middle of the pool, Jupe had recognized the Investigators' business cards sticking out of those comics.

But all their comics with the cards were up in their room—they hadn't sold any.

That meant the comics in that bag had to be the ones stolen out of DeMento's hand in the smoke cloud!

What was this girl doing with them?

10

A Girl of Many Faces

JUPE BURST OUT OF THE WATER AND HAULED HIMSELF FROM the pool. The startled girl sat up in her lounger, staring at him.

He looked into her big hazel eyes and realized he knew his fellow swimmer. Only now she was a brunette instead of a blonde.

"Rainey!" he said furiously. "What are you doing here?"

Rainey Fields glanced around, a look of guilt on her face. "Oh, you're not going to tell, are you? I don't think anyone else has seen . . ."

Jupe looked down at the comics under the chair. "Why should I keep quiet about this?" he demanded.

But Rainey grabbed his hand. "*Please* don't tell," she begged him. "If this gets out, my mother will kill me!"

That was a line Jupe hadn't expected. He kept quiet as Rainey went on. "I thought that nobody would be around this early," she said. "So I figured it was worth the chance to take a swim. But if Mom finds out . . ."

Jupe blinked. Obviously there was a missed connection here. "What are you talking about?" he finally said.

"That stupid blond wig! I wanted to sneak in a quick swim, and I can't wear it in the pool. With my ordinary hair, a plain bathing suit, and no make-up, I didn't think anyone would recognize me. Guess I was wrong."

She sat, hugging herself tight. "I saw you after I was in the water. But you didn't say anything, so I figured I was okay. Just my luck, trying to fool a detective."

Rainey looked up at him pleadingly. "If Mom finds out I've been around out of costume, she'll positively freak! She'll swear I'll never get the job of modeling Stellara Stargirl. She'll—"

"Look," Jupiter cut her off. "I just want you to tell me what these are doing in here."

He picked up the beach bag with the comics and shoved it at her.

"What are you . . . ?" Then Rainey saw the comic books. "What are they doing in here?"

"Yeah, what?" Jupe replied grimly.

"They're not mine." Several emotions chased across Rainey's face. Puzzlement at the strange comics. Relief as she spotted the identifying cards. Then anger as she recognized Jupe's card. "These are yours! They have your cards in them. What are you scaring me for . . . ?"

Then came wide-eyed dismay. "Oh, no. I heard

that some of your comics had been stolen, too. These—these aren't the ones, are they?"

Jupe watched the whole performance. Either Rainey deserved an Oscar, or she was for real. He couldn't see how anyone could have faked those reactions. "Those *are* the missing comics," he said. "More than three hundred dollars' worth. Now, how did they get in your bag?"

Rainey leaned back, looking puzzled, but Jupe noticed her hands had clenched in her lap. "I have no idea," she admitted in a small voice.

Jupe could tell Rainey was beginning to realize her predicament. She was facing more trouble than a lecture from her mom about not wearing her costume. What would being caught with stolen property do to her career?

As she glanced up at him Rainey suddenly looked very vulnerable—and it wasn't just the lack of make-up. "This *is* your bag, isn't it?" Jupe asked a little more quietly.

Rummaging past the comics, Rainey came up with a comb and some sunglasses. "These are mine," she said miserably. "It must be my bag. But I swear I don't know where those comics came from."

"Did you talk to anybody this morning? Or maybe you left your bag out somewhere?" Jupe asked.

Rainey shook her head. "Uh-uh. *Not* seeing anybody was the whole idea. I didn't want anyone to recognize me. And my bag's been with me ever since I left my room."

She shrugged. "Except, of course, for the time I was in the water."

"Of course," Jupe echoed. His muscles tensed as he began to feel angry at himself.

It would be the easiest thing in the world to walk over to Rainey's bag and plant the comics in there. He scanned the quiet poolside. Nobody around—not even a lifeguard.

The only other possible witness was Jupe himself. And he'd been too busy looking at Rainey in her tank suit to notice anyone near the bag. The thief could have marched up with a brass band and planted anything he liked.

Rainey's voice broke into his thoughts. "I guess you want these back," she said timidly, holding out the comics. "They belong to you, after all. But why would anybody stick them in my bag?"

Her puzzled look changed to a grin. "It's like a corny movie where the master spy goofs up and gives the secret formula to the wrong person."

Jupe borrowed her towel to dry off before taking the comic books. Could that be it? Could this have been some kind of drop that went wrong?

"It strains credibility," Jupe said, riffling through the books. "I mean—"

She grinned. "You aren't so mad anymore. You're talking like usual now."

"Um," Jupe said unhappily. "These are all the ones we lost. Could this be the thief's way of dumping the books he didn't want? But why pick you?"

A thought suddenly struck Jupe. He'd already seen Rainey's mother in action. The woman was a born publicity hound. And what could be better publicity than for Rainey to find some of the stolen comics?

Of course, to do that, Ma Fields would have to get her hands on the stolen books. Or have stolen them herself.

He glanced down at Rainey, who looked up at him, all innocence. Certainly Rainey couldn't have done the job. He'd seen her and the Crimson Phantom together. But what about Mrs. Fields? She probably wouldn't even tell her daughter.

Jupe was about to ask a question when an angry voice hissed in his ear. "So this is where you are!"

He turned to find Mrs. Fields glaring past him at Rainey.

"What was the big idea of disappearing like that? I've been tracking you all over this hotel. And what do I find you doing? Sitting here—with one of those so-called detectives."

Jupe got a two-megaton glare from Rainey's mother as the girl quickly assembled her stuff.

"Sorry, Mom," Rainey said meekly.

Her mother thrust out a folding sun hat. "Now hide your hair under that and put on your sunglasses. Maybe no one will notice you."

She grabbed Rainey by the arm and started hauling her off. "Honestly, Rainey, I don't know what gets into you sometimes. I've managed to set up a major television spot for you today. You know we have to get ready. And what do you do? Go off to the pool to ruin your skin with sun and chlorine. Then, to top it off, you break our biggest rule!"

The woman whirled around to glare at Jupe again. "Young man," she said, "I sincerely hope that I don't hear any talk about my daughter's little secret. I'm sure you want to see her successful. If you do anything to hurt her chances, you'll have to deal with me."

Rainey stood behind her mother, looking deeply mortified. But as she was hauled off again, she managed a helpless little grin for Jupe.

As they rushed away Jupe noticed the way Mrs. Fields's clothes billowed as she moved. She was wearing a tentlike dress, almost like a robe.

As he watched the folded fabric move Jupe couldn't help thinking that the figure under the Crimson Phantom's robe didn't necessarily have to be a man.

11

Publicity Fiends

BOB AND PETE WERE ONLY HALF-AWAKE WHEN JUPE BURST back into room 316. But their eyes opened wide when they saw the comics in his hand.

"Where'd you get those?" Pete wanted to know, sitting up in bed.

"Through underwater surveillance," Jupe answered, deadpan. He was about to explain when the phone rang.

Pete picked it up with a "Who could this be?" expression on his face. Then his eyebrows went up as he listened. "For you, Bob. Your father."

"Hi, Dad. What's up?" Bob said after taking the phone. "Uh-huh. Yeah. Okay, I can take care of it." He hung up the phone, then turned to the guys. "Sax Sendler called. He's trying to book a band at a club in Van Nuys, and he needs to get a demo tape up there. Guess who's elected?"

"Look, I'll give you a lift," Pete offered.

"And I'll come along too." Jupe grinned. "Just as easy to tell my story on the way."

"Thanks, guys." Bob got back on the phone. He dialed Sax Sendler's number and told his boss he'd be arriving in about an hour.

Shortly afterward, they were hurrying down the hallway to the elevator. As they passed suite 314 the door opened. A guy with bleached spiky hair came out carrying a huge cardboard carton. "Okay, Axel," he said over his shoulder. "I'll take this stuff downstairs."

He was well behind them when the elevator arrived. "Hey, guys, can you hold that for me?" he called as the Investigators stepped inside.

"Sure." Pete pressed the OPEN button.

The guy hustled in. "Thanks a lot. I didn't want to be stuck holding these—whoa!"

His grip on the box slipped and it started to tip over. Jupe grabbed the box to steady it. He found himself looking inside—at stack after stack of videotapes.

"Thanks again," the young man said. "Could you press LOBBY for me?"

He got off the elevator, holding the box more carefully this time. Jupe, Bob, and Pete continued on down to the underground garage.

They made very good time on the freeways, arriving early at Sax Sendler's combination home/office in Rocky Beach. The talent agent came out the front door wearing his usual football jersey and squinting behind a pair of sunglasses. He handed a small package to Bob. "The guy who owns the club woke me from a sound sleep calling for this tape." He stifled a yawn. "It's unnatural for anyone in this business to be up at this hour."

He smiled as the Investigators each stifled yawns in reply. "Looks like you guys agree. Anyway, the address is on the package, and it shouldn't take you too long. I wouldn't have asked, but it's important."

"That's okay," Pete said. "We weren't doing anything."

"Much," Jupe added under his breath.

They delivered the tape with no problem, but as they drove back to L.A. along the San Diego Freeway they found themselves stuck in traffic.

Pete left the freeway, taking Sepulveda Boulevard as an alternate route. Passing through Santa Monica, he changed the route again, turning onto Pico.

"Don't look now, but I think Pete is taking us somewhere," Bob said.

"Since we were so close, I wanted to take another look at Madman Dan's," Pete admitted. "Something we saw last night has been nagging at me."

They drove along the boulevard until they were passing the comic shop. "There, about halfway down the block," Pete said.

He pulled up beside a battered green van—the same van DeMento had used to bring his comics to the convention the day before. "When we nearly got run down last night, we all thought the van was a different color," Pete said. "Jupe said it was green—and that started me thinking."

"There are lots of green vans in L.A.," Jupe said.

"But we have one easy way of checking." Pete jumped out of the car and ran around to the front of the van. He nodded grimly. "One headlight is cracked. We've found our Cyclops."

The rest of the ride back was a long, puzzled discussion. "If the van that nearly creamed us is DeMento's, that means he had to be the one who broke into our room," Bob said. "Why'd he do that? We're working for him, aren't we?"

"Maybe we're only providing a cover for him," Jupe said.

Bob gave him a sharp look. "You mean he's the one who stole the comics—and he hired three dumb teenagers to make himself look innocent." He nodded. "And he has a perfect motive—publicity."

"Everybody in the convention must have heard about the robbery at Madman Dan's stall," Jupe agreed. "I'll bet they all went over there to check it out."

Pete shook his head in admiration. "Well, he was ready for them. We saw all the extra stock he moved in yesterday." Then he frowned. "But we saw him there during the robbery. he couldn't have been the Crimson Phantom."

"No, but his assistant could," Jupe pointed out. "DeMento sent him away. A little while later the Crimson Phantom shows up to steal those books."

"That wraps it up nice and neat," said Pete. "Just one question: Can you accuse someone of stealing his own stuff?"

Bob shrugged. "I wouldn't bother. Why give him any more free publicity?" A wicked grin spread across his face. "If we really want to rattle his cage, let's show him the comics that mysteriously turned up again."

Jupe laughed, then got serious. "It might be a good idea. Depending on how he reacts, we can decide if he *is* the thief or whether we continue looking. Why don't we get the comics and bring them to the convention floor?"

They reached the hotel and headed back to their room. This time as they passed suite 314, Axel Griswold himself came out. "I've been looking for you guys! Is it true? I keep hearing that Rainey Fields found the stolen comics."

"Some of them—the ones that belonged to us." Jupe couldn't help grinning at the question. Ma Fields' publicity machine had to be running on overdrive!

As if reading Jupe's mind, Griswold shook his head. "Rainey's mother has been talking of nothing else. Her little TV spot has become a big deal now. By the way, she was looking for you. She wants to borrow the comics so Rainey can hold them for the camera."

He snickered. "There'll be a few news people there, but she's treating the whole thing like a remake of *Gone with the Wind.*"

"Do you think she's going to burn down the hotel for the grand finale?" Jupe asked.

"Maybe that's the threat she used to twist the manager's arm." Griswold leaned forward. "I don't know how she did it, but she arranged for a special elevator for her daughter, complete with uniformed bellhop. Rainey will ride down to her audience in style."

He looked up suddenly. "There she is," he said. "Just think—she came to this convention a Stargirl, but she'll be leaving a star."

Jupe saw Rainey pass by, heading for the elevator. The tall girl was back in her Stellara Stargirl costume. When she saw Jupe, she gave him a nervous little smile. To Jupe's eyes it looked as though Rainey were fighting a major case of stage fright. He also noticed she was alone.

"I guess Mom is downstairs priming all the reporters," Griswold said. "Well, thanks, guys. At least now I know she isn't telling outright lies."

He went back into his room, leaving behind a ripe smell of sour grapes. Why? Jupe wondered. Isn't this great publicity for the convention?

"Do you guys mind if we lend Rainey the comics for this TV thing?" he asked abruptly.

Pete shrugged.

"Sure, why not?" said Bob.

They went into their room, grabbed the pile of comics, then headed back to the elevator.

Rainey was a solitary figure in front of her private elevator. She carefully adjusted her blue cape. She kept staring at the doors as if she could will them to open for her ride to fame. Or was she hoping they'd stay shut?

Jupe was about ten feet from her when the elevator chimes rang out.

"Hey, Rainey," he called, holding up the comics he'd gotten for her.

She turned around, glad to see a friendly face.

That was why she didn't notice anything was wrong with the elevator.

Instead of the usual brightly lit cab, the doors had opened on darkness.

And the arms that reached out to grab Rainey weren't in any bellhop's uniform.

12

Jupe to the Rescue

JUPE TORE TOWARD THE ELEVATOR WITH PETE AND BOB AT his heels. They got there just as the doors closed in their faces. The solid steel cut off Rainey's voice in midscream.

Still clutching the comics in his hands, Jupe whipped around, white-faced. "Come on!"

He ran to the service stairs they'd used on their wild chase of last night's intruder. Tearing open the door, he plunged down the steps at top speed.

Jupe thought he'd never moved so fast. Even Pete was having a tough time keeping up with him. And Bob made a poor third.

Jupe's legs began to ache as he whirled around another landing. Can we catch up with Rainey? he wondered. She's in a high-speed elevator.

But he kept moving as fast as he could, jumping the stairs two and three at a time.

They reached the lobby floor, but Jupe kept going downward. No way was the kidnapper going to come out of the elevator in front of all those TV cameras.

Nor could he risk taking the elevator to one of the other floors. Someone might be standing at the elevator bank, waiting for a ride.

No, the safest place for this guy to head was the nice quiet parking garage. Just the place to bring a struggling victim.

Jupe flew down the last flight of stairs. Just like the night before he hit the panic bar on the door. This time, however, he was moving so fast the door swung as if it had been blasted open.

Jupe *had* to move fast. If that guy got Rainey into a car before they reached him . . .

He dashed for the elevator bank. The sounds of scuffling and muffled screams were almost welcome. They meant Rainey was still there—and still fighting.

"C'mon, kid, stop being stupid. I don't want to hurt you. Just tell me where you hid my stuff, and there'll be no problems."

That voice was familiar. And as he came round in front of the elevators Jupe saw he was right. Dragging Rainey along in a choke hold was Dan DeMento.

A flutter of paper in the face was the first hint to DeMento that he had company. It was the fistful of comics Jupe still held in his hand.

Jupe couldn't have hoped for a more successful diversion. DeMento jumped, then half-turned in surprise. His arm loosened its hold around Rainey's neck.

That was all Jupe needed. He literally tore DeMento away from the girl, hurling him into a concrete wall. The comics dealer hit the wall with a thud and wavered for a second, stunned.

Rainey tottered toward Jupe, about to fall.

Jupe turned and reached out to catch her. DeMento jumped at him. Jupe met the attack with a straight-arm blow that sent DeMento bouncing back to the wall.

Bob caught the swaying Rainey, while Pete moved in to help Jupe finish the job of subduing DeMento. In seconds they had him pinned to the wall.

"Not so easy when you have to fight guys instead of a girl, is it?" Jupe yelled in the comic dealer's face.

He forced his anger back, which wasn't so easy. Especially when he heard Rainey saying in a quavery voice, "Oh, Bob, you saved me!"

About the most serious thing Bob had saved her from was a scraped knee. But this wasn't the time to tell Rainey that. She was still too shaken up by the attack.

"You're okay now," Jupe told Rainey. "We'll take care of that creep."

Rainey gradually calmed down. Then a thought suddenly struck her. "They're waiting for me upstairs!" she exclaimed. "Mom will kill—"

Abruptly she went down on one knee, picking up the comics that Jupe had thrown. She glanced over at Jupe, then looked back at the floor. "Thank you, guys. All of you." She took a deep breath, then asked Bob, "Do I look all right? I've got to go up."

"You look fine," Bob assured her. "Go on."

"I don't think I'll mention what happened down here," Rainey said. "I'll talk to you about it later."

Jupe heard her get back in the elevator. He couldn't bear to look. How typical. After all his worrying, his fighting—*Bob* becomes her hero.

Once again Jupe had to swallow his anger. Then he thought of a more constructive use for it. There was a lot to be shaken out of Dan DeMento.

"We've got to stop meeting like this," Bob said to DeMento.

"Wha—what do you mean?" DeMento's hair was wilder than ever. He shook his head, still trying to get over being knocked around.

"You mean you've forgotten all about last night?" Jupe asked. "When you nearly ran all three of us down?"

"With your nice green van," Pete added, taking Jupe's cue. "The one with the broken headlight."

"I didn't mean to—I mean . . ."

"What *do* you mean?" Jupe pressed DeMento hard. "Burglary, trying to kill us, kidnapping that girl . . ."

"It wasn't that way at all!" DeMento insisted, his voice shaking. "I heard that the girl in the gold outfit had found the stolen comics. Then the story changed—she'd only found *your* comics. That sounded fishy to me."

He squinted angrily. "I saw her by my stall right before the comics got stolen. Now she was suddenly 'finding' some of them. I figured she must have them all. And I wanted to get her alone, to find out where she'd hidden them. So I got rid of the bellhop for a minute and borrowed his elevator."

For a horrible second Jupe wondered if they had just let the real thief make her escape on the elevator. No. Rainey's surprise and shock at finding the books had been genuine. "You picked the wrong person, DeMento. I was there when she found the comics. Somebody had slipped them into her bag."

"I had to do *something*!" For a moment Madman Dan looked like a real madman as he pleaded with Jupe. "I've been going nuts ever since that guy ripped me off. And it didn't look like you guys were coming up with much. So I started poking around on my own. That's why I went to that room last night."

"You wanted to search *our* room?" Pete asked.

"I didn't even know you guys were in there. All I knew was that it was connected to 314, and I wanted to get into the suite to search—"

"Axel Griswold?" Bob's voice was disbelieving.

"Axel Griswold's *stock*." Jupe tapped his forehead with his fist. "That guy with the box of videotapes who came out of Griswold's room this morning. I should have remembered where I'd seen him. He was the one selling the hot tapes at the Kamikaze Komics stall."

Jupe looked at Dan DeMento, who had calmed down a little when he saw he wasn't about to be lynched.

"What's the connection between Griswold and Kamikaze Komics?" Jupe asked.

"He owns the place," Madman Dan answered

promptly. "Didn't you know? That's how he got into running these conventions. He's been a comics dealer for years."

"A comics dealer for years," Jupe repeated, trying to fit this new information in with all the rest they'd gathered.

One thing was certain, at least. Dan DeMento could not be the thief.

The robbery itself, even the break-in at the Investigators' room, could be explained as publicity gimmicks. But kidnapping a girl was not the kind of publicity a sane person would want.

Jupe sighed. He'd just lost a suspect. And he found himself back at square one again.

There was one question he wanted to ask DeMento, though.

"When we saw you with that replacement issue of *Fan Fun*, the price sticker said two hundred and fifty dollars. Yet when Leo Rottweiler tried to buy the one that was stolen, you quoted six hundred dollars and he actually considered paying it. What makes that copy so valuable?"

A crafty smirk spread over Dan DeMento's face. "It was autographed by Steve Tresh," he explained. "A real collector's item. A Steve Tresh original."

13

Rainey Shows Her Hand

"AUTOGRAPHED?" JUPE SAID. "I DON'T COLLECT COMICS, and even I know Steve Tresh doesn't sign any Crimson Phantom stuff. Frank Carne told me the whole story. I even saw Tresh refusing to sign art for the fans."

"You're absolutely right," DeMento said, his smirk growing bigger under his unruly mustache. "But this is *Fan Fun*—and the *Gray* Phantom. It came out long before *The Crimson Phantom*. I figure Tresh must have autographed the book before all the trouble began. And it was all mine."

The smirk abruptly disappeared. "It *was* all mine. Until some creep stole it."

Jupe frowned in thought. "You never got a chance to show that book to Tresh, did you?"

Madman Dan shook his head. "I didn't even meet him until after the book was stolen. And instead of talking about the book, I wound up going after Frank Carne."

He looked at the Three Investigators and cleared his

throat. "Uh, guys, what are you going to do about me?"

"Oh, you mean about last night?" Jupe asked. "That little business of breaking and entering, assault, and reckless endangerment?"

"Yeah." DeMento was really sweating now. "That business."

Jupe shrugged. "The only thing we could go to the police and prove is a traffic violation. You should get your headlight fixed."

DeMento relaxed a little.

Then Bob spoke up. "But Rainey Fields will have to make up her own mind about what happened today. She said she wanted to talk with us about it. Maybe you should be deciding what *you'll* say."

That's right, Jupe thought. Rainey would be coming back to talk to them.

"I really should be heading upstairs to my stall," DeMento said. He gave them a wry smile. "You know where to find me. Maybe you could bring her over. Whatever happens, I should give her an explanation—and an apology."

"Sounds good to me," Pete said, pushing the elevator button. "So, what do we do next?"

"Let's try and find Steve Tresh," Jupe said promptly. "I want to talk about autographs."

They rode up to the lobby together and headed for the main conference room. There was a small line of stragglers at the table by the entrance getting hand stamps from the girl with the two-toned hair.

DeMento hurried off toward his stall. As Bob, Pete, and Jupe tried to enter, however, the husky security guard blocked their path. "Sorry, guys, that stamp looks awful faded."

He peered at the backs of their hands and gave them his chip-toothed grin. "Just like I thought. Yesterday's stamp. Nice try, guys."

Jupe reached for his wallet. "I knew there was something else we were supposed to do this morning."

A few moments later, with INTERCOMICON—DAY 2 stamped on their hands, the Investigators were plowing through the crowd on the convention floor.

"Next stop, Steve Tresh," Pete said, looking around. "Where do you think we'll find him?"

"I think our first shot should be the artists' tables," Jupe suggested. "If he's not there, at least someone might be able to tell us where he went."

Tresh's seat was empty, and there were no hopeful fans around his table. Worse still, none of the artists knew where he was. "He left a while ago," said an older man, carefully inking in a pencil sketch of Wacky Wodent. "Didn't say anything. Just went."

"Any other ideas?" Bob asked Jupe.

"When in doubt, try the hotel reception desk," Jupe answered.

"No, I'm afraid Mr. Tresh can't be reached," the reception clerk told Jupe. "He's in an important meeting."

"Did he say when he'd be available?" Jupe asked.

"Sometime this afternoon," she said.

"Could I leave a message for him?" Jupe took a pen and paper from the clerk, scribbled a brief note, and handed it back to her. "I asked him to meet us at DeMento's stall," he told the others.

"Well, now we know where we'll spend the afternoon," Pete responded.

Madman Dan looked nervous when he saw the Investigators coming toward him. "Did you talk to the girl yet?" he asked.

He relaxed a bit when Jupe explained what they were doing there. "Sure. Anything I can do to help. I suppose you want Tresh to talk to me anyway."

Just then a kid came staggering up. He was almost invisible behind a huge cardboard carton, which was about three times the size of the comic box the Investigators had left in their room. "Excuse me, guys," DeMento said. "This looks like business."

The kid dropped his box to the floor and peered up at Madman Dan suspiciously. "Think we can do a trade?" he whined, leaning heavily against the table. "I'm trying to get *Slime Man* Number One. I've got Number One and Number Two of *The Outrageous Ooze.*"

DeMento nodded. "Sounds like a pretty fair trade."

He turned to the back rack of the stall and reached for *Slime Man.*

At the same time, the kid hoisted the box up and dropped it sharply on the edge of the table.

DeMento was just in the act of handing over the comic. "Here you—watch out!" The table collapsed.

"Gosh, I'm sorry. Let me help clean up." The kid got down on his knees, picking up the comics that had fallen off the table. DeMento and his assistant were busy getting the folding table to stand up again.

The kid left the comics in a big pile, then started pushing his box away.

Madman Dan planted a foot in his way. "Just a second," he said, pulling the carton open. He quickly plucked out a comic. "Here's my copy of *Slime Man*. I wonder how it got in there?" He shook the comic in the kid's face. "No deal, kid. Beat it, and don't come back."

The kid disappeared quickly, considering the size of the box he had to lug away.

Madman Dan watched him go, shaking his head. "He's probably got a few more of my comics in there. That's why I keep the money stuff in the back—and only cheapies on the front table."

He laughed. "And Frank Carne thinks *I'm* a crook."

The mention of Frank Carne's name sparked a thought in Jupe's mind. This little sideshow had just eliminated Frank the Crank as a suspect. While the Crimson Phantom's billowing robe might have concealed his identity, there was no way a person of his bulk could have vaulted over the table. Not without bringing it to the floor. But could the Phantom have been Mrs. Fields?

"Hi, guys."

Jupe turned to see Rainey Fields holding out a stack

of comic books. "I saw you over here and figured I should return these," she said.

"Uh—thanks." Jupe tucked the pile under his arm, a little embarrassed to think he'd just been suspecting Rainey's mother. "How did your interviews go?"

"Fine. Mom told me that I was finally learning showmanship—making them wait a minute before making my entrance. If she knew the *real* reason . . ." She shuddered, her eyes flicking over to Dan DeMento. "I guess it's time to talk."

DeMento kept nervously stacking and restacking comics. "I want to say I'm sorry," he began. "I made a big mistake."

By the time Madman Dan had finished his explanation, Rainey had accepted his apology. Then she turned to Jupe. "I owe *you* an apology, too."

Jupe stared in surprise as she went on. "You were the one who jumped in and saved me—and I didn't really thank you." Her eyes shone. "I never saw anyone fight like that before."

"Oh, uh, yeah." Jupe could feel his face turning bright red as Rainey patted his hand.

"Thank you."

"Well, uh, why don't, uh . . ." Jupe couldn't understand it. All of a sudden his tongue felt glued to the roof of his mouth. He could feel Pete and Bob staring at him.

Finally he took Rainey by the arm and led her a few steps away. "Why don't we go out and have lunch?" Amazing. The words came out sounding halfway normal.

"Okay." Rainey leaned forward, a conspiratorial glint in her eyes. "I'll meet you in the garden by the side entrance—twenty minutes."

Then she was gone.

Jupe could not believe his luck. He turned back to his friends. "I'm having lunch with Rainey. You guys don't mind, do you?"

"Oh, no." Bob shook his head. "And even if I did, you'd probably smooth-talk me into changing my mind."

"Right," said Pete. "I've got to remember that line. 'Well, uh, why don't, uh. . . .' "

"Thanks, guys," Jupe muttered as he headed for their room to drop off the comics and neaten up. "Thanks a lot."

Jupe didn't know what to expect as he waited in the garden. What he got was Rainey in shorts and a T-shirt, with her short brown hair. She looked normal, everyday—and gorgeous.

"Is this your secret identity?" he asked.

Rainey grinned. "You've got it." She linked her arm through his and led him onto the sidewalk. She was a bit taller than Jupe's 5 feet 8¾ inches, but Jupe didn't even care.

"I'm glad for a chance to get out of that crazy costume," Rainey went on. "And I know this great place nearby—burgers and salads and stuff. Where nobody cares about Stellara Stargirl."

The restaurant was light and airy, with lots of glass, lots of plants—and lots of alfalfa sprouts, as Jupe quickly found out. Rainey ordered the same salad as Jupe, eating it with much more enjoyment than he did.

But then she hadn't had to live on alfalfa sprouts for two weeks. When he'd read the book on this diet, it had seemed like an easy way to lose weight. Now he was getting awfully tired of sprouts—and he was about twenty-five miles behind on his walking.

Rainey had the Investigators' card out and was reading it. "You really investigate crimes?" she said.

He shrugged. "We've done it for years."

"And you're the founder. The other two guys are your associates." She looked up at him.

"That is what it says on the card." A big clump of sprouts dropped from Jupe's fork onto the table. He quickly shoved it under his plate. Oh, great, he thought. Now that I've got my mouth working, my hands begin to shake.

"It must be great to have a team like that. Your big friend—Pete? He looks pretty strong."

Jupe nodded. "Yeah. He's a real jock."

Rainey leaned forward on the table. "And your other friend—Bob. What's he like?"

Another forkful of sprouts landed on the table. Jupe sighed. He should have seen this coming.

For the rest of the lunch Jupe talked about some of the criminals they'd put away—and Bob. Weird clues they'd discovered—and Bob. Tough cases they'd cracked—and, of course, Bob. Jupe only managed to steer the conversation away from Bob for a few brief minutes, when he got Rainey to talk about herself.

"Why do you go around in that crazy costume?" he asked.

"It's kind of hard to explain," Rainey said. "I've always liked comics. Mom didn't really appreciate that—until she saw Stellara Stargirl and figured this could get me started as a model."

"Is that what you want to do?"

"Nah." Rainey laughed. "I want to be a comic artist."

Jupe started laughing too. "Drawing Slime Man?"

"Not exactly. But it might be fun to have a girl drawing Stellara Stargirl."

After that, Jupe couldn't think of anything else to say. When the time came to pay for lunch, he was almost glad.

They were back in the garden by the hotel's side entrance. "Thanks. I had a nice time," Rainey told him.

"Yeah, uh, nice." Jupe's tongue seemed to have gotten itself disconnected again. He took a step forward.

"I'll see you around. Will you be staying through tomorrow?" As she spoke Rainey stuck out her hand.

Jupe stared at her hand. Oh, no. She was going to shake hands. A humiliating lunch and a good-bye *handshake*.

"I don't know how long we'll be here. Until we

clear up this case." Jupe decided he might as well get the handshake over with. He took her hand. "Take it easy . . . Hey!"

"What?" Rainey tried to pull her hand away, but Jupe wouldn't let go. He kept turning their right hands back and forth, staring at the black letters stamped on the back.

"Jupe," she said, "what are you doing?"

"Realizing something that I should have noticed a long time ago."

"Something you saw at the robbery?"

He patted the back of her hand. "Something I *didn't* see. When the Crimson Phantom dropped those smoke bombs, I saw the backs of both his hands."

"So?" Rainey said.

"So," Jupe answered, "neither of them was stamped."

14

A Dead Deal

STILL HOLDING RAINEY'S HAND, JUPE RUSHED TOWARD THE door. "We've got to see the guys and let them know about this."

"Hold it!" Rainey finally yanked her hand free. "I can't go on the convention floor looking like this. Somebody might recognize me. And if that happens, my mom—"

"Will kill you," Jupe finished for her.

"Besides, what's so important about our hands?" she asked.

"It proves the robbery was an inside job," Jupe explained. "You, me, the dealers—*anybody* who came into the convention had to get their hands stamped—an indelible ticket we had to show at the door. But the person who dropped those smoke bombs had clean hands. No stamp. How did he get in? He couldn't—unless he was working here."

"I see what you mean." Rainey hesitated, looking across the lobby toward the elevator bank. "Look, I want to help on this case, if I can. After all, I'm involved now. Let me go upstairs and get back into costume. I'll meet you at Madman Dan's booth."

"Want me to walk you to your room?" Jupe asked.

Rainey grinned. "No. I think I'll be safe on the elevator this time."

Jupe headed back to the main conference room, presenting his hand with a flourish to the gorilla security guard. He made his way through the crowd to Madman Dan's stall. Standing in front of it were Bob and Pete.

"Did Stellara Stargirl take you over to the next galaxy for lunch?" Pete asked.

"Is there anything you want to tell us?" Bob's voice sounded serious, but he kept waggling his eyebrows at Jupe. "Have you learned anything new about life?"

"I discovered a clue while you guys were thinking up gags," Jupe said. "Has Steve Tresh showed up yet?"

"Somebody mention my name?" asked Steve Tresh as he walked up to the stall. "Good timing," the sandy-haired artist said with a smile. "I just got here myself, and I'm ready for a celebration." He tapped the pocket of his jacket. "In here is a contract signed with an independent distributor. My new comic will be shipped nationwide as soon as it gets off the press."

"Which distributor?" Dan DeMento asked.

"Ned Root. He was in town for the convention, so we did our business right in his suite. Hush-hush stuff. I had to sneak away for our meetings."

"Is that where you were when Dan got robbed?" Jupe asked.

Tresh nodded. "After I'd made my first presentation to Ned, I came down to the convention floor and found it full of smoke. I guess you guys know the rest."

"Did anyone know about your negotiations?"

"Nobody. Like I said. I wasn't going to ruin the *Major Mayhem* deal by blabbing around about it."

"*Major Mayhem?*" DeMento broke in, his mustache quivering. "What kind of a hero is he? A wrestler? A GI? A mercenary? A rock star?"

Tresh gave him a sly smile. "You'll just have to buy the first issue and see." He looked at Jupe. "Why did you ask if anyone knew about the negotiations?"

Jupe lowered his voice. "I've been thinking about what's happened to you—the destruction of your artwork and the attack last night. Whoever did it to you obviously didn't know you had a strong reason to stick around."

Bob leaned forward. "Jupe, this keeps getting heavier and heavier. You make it sound like somebody is trying to drive Steve away."

"That's exactly what I'm trying to say." Jupe looked at Tresh. "If you didn't have to stay for this distribution deal, would you have hung around?"

"No way—not even to make my speech," the artist admitted. "I was beginning to think Rottweiler had somehow gotten wind of the negotiations and was trying to wreck them. But you said—"

"The person *didn't* know about the impending deal," Jupe said. "Otherwise I expect Mr. Root would have been having problems too. The attacks were aimed directly at you, Steve, and I believe they're tied up somehow with that stolen copy of *Fan Fun*. They *have* to be."

He looked over at DeMento. "Why don't you ask him about that autograph?"

"Autograph?" Tresh looked wary. "I hope you're not going to ask me to sign some stupid piece of—"

"This is about something you already signed," DeMento said quickly.

"*May* have signed," Jupe added.

"What?" Tresh still looked suspicious.

"I've seen you refuse to autograph artwork from your Heroic Comics days," Jupe said. "I've even seen you burn it."

"Oh, you caught that little act, too." Now Tresh was becoming embarrassed. "I guess I got a little carried away there. But I think I had good reason. Heroic Comics, and especially Leo Rottweiler, gave me a really raw deal."

"We know," Jupe said. "Frank the Crank told us all about it."

The artist jammed his hands into his pockets. "Well, there's no way I'm going to help their business along by autographing my old artwork."

"You weren't always angry at Heroic Comics," DeMento pointed out. "How about the time before you quit? You must have autographed stuff then."

Tresh laughed. "Back then Heroic was giving me so much work doing art and scripts, I was too busy to sign my own name. Or too tired."

"And before that?" DeMento went on. "Your *Fan Fun* days."

"What? Oh, you mean the Gray Phantom story." Tresh shook his head. "I wasn't famous enough to sign autographs back then. Who cares about an unknown artist?"

"Well, maybe you forgot about it, but you must have signed one," DeMento insisted. "For your mother, or your girlfriend, a buddy . . . maybe someone you were working with."

"I think I would have remembered signing a Gray Phantom story." Tresh frowned. "What's this about?"

"I had a copy of *Fan Fun* with your autograph." Madman Dan was absolutely sure.

"You couldn't. I never signed any." Tresh sounded equally positive.

"Look, it was your name. Right across the splash page of your story."

Tresh's eyes narrowed. "If only I could see it."

"But of course you can't," Jupe said. "The robbery took care of that."

The artist turned to DeMento. "Do you remember what the autograph looked like?" he asked. "My signature has changed a lot from those days. We could tell if somebody copied an autograph from something more recent. Because I sure don't remember ever signing that book."

"Maybe it's one you don't want to remember," DeMento said. "Because the guy who sold it to me would certainly know your signature."

"Who was it?" Pete asked.

"Leo Rottweiler."

The Investigators stared at DeMento in disbelief.

"That snake!" Tresh burst out. "I wouldn't give him the time of day, much less an autograph."

"I thought it was something he had from when you were still friendly—when you were working together," DeMento said.

"Our working days were never exactly friendly." Tresh smiled bitterly. "He was the old pro, the big editor, and I was the kid starting out. He gave *me* an autograph once. When I left Heroic, I burned the dumb thing."

"So where did Rottweiler get the book?" asked Bob.

"I don't know," Tresh replied. "But it wasn't from me."

With a swirl of blue cape and a glitter of gold costume, Rainey rushed up. "Did I miss anything?"

"No," Jupe said. "You're just in time for the fireworks. We're going to have a chat with Leo Rottweiler."

"I'd like to punch him in the mouth," Tresh muttered.

"Well, I wouldn't hold you back," DeMento said to him. "He's responsible for the latest cute trick from Heroic. They're reprinting old issues of their successful books as Heroic Classics."

"You mean he's reprinting the stuff we used to read?" Pete said.

DeMento nodded. "Especially your stuff, Steve. Crimson Phantom Classics will take in big bucks. Of course," he went on bitterly, "it drives down the value of the original books. And I'm stuck with a bunch of them, taking a loss."

"Is that why you gave Rottweiler such a hard time when he tried to buy *Fan Fun* back?" Jupe asked.

"Yeah," said DeMento, smiling. "He pestered me for days, but I wouldn't give him the satisfaction."

"Well, gentlemen, let's see what Mr. Rottweiler has to say," said Jupe.

They reached the Heroic Comics area, which was set up for another press conference. Leo Rottweiler smiled at Rainey. His smile faded when he noticed who was following her.

"Tresh!" He gave the artist a thin smile. "Come to make more ridiculous accusations?"

"No, we've just come to ask a few questions." Jupe was the soul of courtesy. "We're all interested in that collector's item you were trying to buy back."

"Buy back? I don't know what you're talking about," the balding editor blustered, but his eyes began darting around nervously when he saw Dan DeMento.

"You know. That copy of *Fan Fun* Number One you tried to buy from Mr. DeMento here." Jupe went on as if Rottweiler had never spoken. "He told us that you were the one who originally sold it to him."

"What has that got to do with anything?" Two small red dots appeared over Rottweiler's cheeks. "I won't put up with another half-baked accusation!"

"Oh, we know you didn't *steal* the book," Jupe cut him off. "You were with Frank Carne outside the

Gold Room when the smoke bombs went off. What we wanted to know was why you were so anxious to buy the fanzine back."

"I, ah, got a much better offer for the book, and saw the chance to make a profit. Nothing wrong with that, is there?"

Jupe nodded. "But you couldn't make the deal, could you?"

"No." Rottweiler pointed a shaking finger at DeMento. "Because *he* kept pushing the price impossibly high, until, ah, my prospective buyer cut it off."

"So who was the prospective buyer?" Pete asked.

Rottweiler licked his lips.

"It's a dead deal, Mr. Rottweiler," Bob spoke up. "Why don't you tell us who wanted it?"

"Kamikaze Komics." Rottweiler had a trapped look on his face as he answered.

"Where did you get the book in the first place?" Tresh asked. "I know it wasn't from me."

Rottweiler gave up completely. "Kamikaze Komics," he muttered.

"I don't think we have to disturb Mr. Rottweiler any more," Jupe said.

The group filed out of the stall.

"Very, *very* interesting," Jupe said. "An inside job. A store that sells a comic and suddenly wants it back. Things are finally coming together. A few more answers and we should have our thief." He smiled and sped up the aisle. "And I know just where to look."

15

Big Shop of Horrors

JUPE VEERED OFF TO THE LEFT SO SHARPLY THAT HE almost lost the rest of his parade in the crowd.

"Hold on. Where are we going?" Rainey asked as she caught up with him.

"Where all the problems in this convention seem to come from." He stopped across the aisle from the Kamikaze Komics stall.

There was no way the Investigators and their friends could get any closer. The crowd at the stall was the densest they'd seen that weekend—literally wall-to-wall bodies.

"You'd think they were giving out things for free," Bob said.

"They just about are," one red-faced, happy collector told him. "These tapes were going for thirty bucks yesterday. I got this for ten!"

"That's still much more than the tape is really worth," Jupe whispered. Yet he found himself intrigued. Why were they selling everything off?

He plunged into the crowd to find out. After several

minutes of dodging through wriggling bodies and thumping elbows, he reached the counter. The Kamikaze crew was really hopping, serving up comics and videotapes at real discounts. "Okay, sport, what are you looking for?" the blond spiky-haired guy asked Jupe.

"Um—*Stellara Stargirl*?" It was the first comic name to enter Jupe's mind.

"Good choice! We've got a special here, numbers one through five, all wrapped together. Usually fifty dollars"—he looked at Jupe appraisingly—"for you, fifteen."

Jupe had no choice but to shell out the money. As he did he looked at the guy's hands. No, he hadn't been the Crimson Phantom. His fingers were stubby, the nails bitten, and the stamp was prominent on the back of his hand.

Jupe's eyes flicked to the other salesmen's hands as his change was counted out. None fit the bill.

"There you go. Thanks!" The guy turned to one of the workers. "Hey, Jerry, we need some more of the special merchandise."

"This?" The guy pulled out another package of *Stellara Stargirl* comics. Jupe noticed that the cover price was ten bucks.

"No, stupid, the *special* merchandise. They'd better bring it over from the store. We've got some live ones here."

Jupe fought his way free of the mob scene and rejoined his group. Rainey began to laugh when she saw what he'd bought. "You can autograph them for me later," Jupe told her. "We have a little field trip now."

"Field trip? Where?" DeMento asked.

"Kamikaze Komics. They're selling a lot of this junk." Jupe waved his packaged set. "But they have some kind of special merchandise over at the store. I wonder if it's so special that they had to steal it back."

"And you want to see what's there. Well, I've got a van." Madman Dan shrugged his shoulders. "My assistant will just have to mind my stall until we get back."

"I'm coming too," Rainey announced. She looked down at her gold outfit. "But I don't think I'm dressed right . . ."

"Here." Tresh gave her his jacket. "We might need a superperson down in that neighborhood."

They went to the parking garage and took off—Tresh, Rainey, and Madman Dan in the green van, the Investigators in Pete's Impala.

"You're sure you know where this store is?" Jupe asked as they pulled up the ramp.

"DeMento said it was on Hollywood near Western," Pete answered. "He said we couldn't miss it."

He was right—they *couldn't* miss it. Kamikaze Komics had the ground floor of an old four-story building, but they'd painted the whole front into an ad for the store. Against a blinding yellow background flying superheroes battled Japanese Zeros. "Kamikaze Komics." Bob laughed. "What else?"

They parked, then gathered at the van to discuss strategy. "You know, I used to hang out here all the time when I started collecting comics," DeMento said. "They had the cheapest prices."

"And the lowest rent," Tresh added, looking around the shabby neighborhood.

"Back then," DeMento went on, "the basement of the shop sold secondhand paperbacks. Now it's used for storage. Whatever we're looking for should be down there." DeMento looked around the group. "I know where the cellar stairs are, but they'll stop us unless we have a distraction."

Rainey grinned and opened Steve Tresh's jacket. "I think I can take care of that."

Moments later they put their hastily developed plan into action. During the next five minutes Tresh, DeMento, and Jupe wandered in, acting like casual customers. Five minutes after that, Rainey was to follow. Bob and Pete would stay outside, ready to come in as reinforcements if anything went wrong.

Jupe had half-expected to find the same booming business he'd seen at the convention stall. But Kamikaze Komics was like a ghost town—two bored-looking clerks and maybe four customers with their noses buried in the comics racks.

The dingy walls had once been much more densely stocked. Jupe could see clean squares in the dust where whole boxes had been removed. It's beginning to look like a going-out-of-business sale, he thought. But it seems to be happening awfully fast.

He glanced around and spotted DeMento. He was standing by a door in the rear of the store. The big clean-out had actually helped them. A lot of boxes had been cleared out of that area, opening it up. Jupe walked over, occasionally taking a look at a comic. Tresh worked his way over too.

Then the front door opened and Rainey walked in, her costume shining and a big grin on her face. She had the same effect she'd had at the convention. Every head turned toward her.

Except for Jupe, Tresh, and DeMento. Madman Dan eased open the basement door, and the three of them zipped down the stairs. A dusty forty-watt bulb hung over the stairway, casting a feeble glow.

Jupe looked for a light switch as he, DeMento, and Tresh reached the bottom. No luck. Not that there was so much to see in the dimness. Just a small pile of boxes and a big pile of disassembled machinery.

Jupe stared at the pieces. Somewhere he'd seen a machine like this. Where? Slowly the memory came together. The salvage yard. Uncle Titus coming back from a closed-down print shop. "You know what this is?" Jupe whispered. "An old offset printing press. But what were they printing?"

He stepped forward, and his toe hit a crumpled wad of paper. It skittered across the floor toward Tresh, who picked it up and straightened it out. "Hey, Dan," he said, "know what this is?"

The page was crudely printed in black and white. It looked like a collection of daily comic strips.

"Sure." DeMento peered at it. "In the early days they used to reprint newspaper comics into black-and-white yearly books. That page must be fifty years old."

"I think this is a newer reprint." Tresh pointed at the page. "This pulp paper should be yellow and brittle. It should have split when I unfolded it."

"Well, now we know what the 'specials' are," Jupe said. "Counterfeit comics."

"Yeah," said a voice from the doorway. "So now what do we do with you?"

They looked up the stairway. Three figures were silhouetted against the lights of the store. One stepped forward into the dim glow of the stair light. Jupe recognized him then—the beefy security guard from the convention entrance.

"I thought you guys would have gotten the hint when your big pal went flying without wings. But no, Fat Boy's got to go around asking questions, Skinny has to stick his nose where it's not wanted, and Big Guy's still leading with his chin." He grinned down at them, showing his chipped tooth. "I hope you're not thinking about hollering or anything. We just closed the store. And the walls here are pretty thick."

"Purvis," one of the store clerks said nervously, "what are we supposed to do?"

"Yeah, Purvis," Jupe asked. "What *are* you supposed to do? How'd you know we were here?"

"That dippy Rottfink guy came squealing to the boss that you'd been asking questions about us. He figured you'd be coming to the store." He grinned again. "And he sent me here to take care of you three."

He can't see us clearly in the dark, Jupe realized. He thinks DeMento and Tresh are Pete and Bob. "I bet you do a lot of 'taking care' for Axel Griswold," he said aloud, stepping forward into the light. Behind his back he signaled the others to stay in the dimness.

"I remember now—the girl who stamped hands was checking them at the convention entrance when Pete got knocked off the balcony. Were you off on a break? Or off breaking into Steve Tresh's room?" Jupe hoped that Tresh would control his temper. Their only hope was to play for time until Pete and Bob decided to bust in. And what had happened to Rainey up there?

"You were also there at the dinner, breaking up the fight between Tresh and Rottweiler. Did you go out afterward and finish up with Tresh—alone?"

Purvis waggled his head. "You know, I can see why the boss is beginning to get worried about you guys. You've figured out a lot. Too much."

"Not all of it, though. I thought you might have turned out to be the Crimson Phantom, but you don't have the right hands. Too pudgy." They were running out of time. Purvis and his friends were about to make their move.

"Too pudgy, huh?" Purvis said. "You'll find out soon enough—real soon."

Jupe braced himself. "You're awfully sure of the way this will turn out. After all, it's three against three."

Purvis gave them his chipped-tooth smile again. "Yeah, but we make sure we win."

From behind his back he brought out a baseball bat, tapping the fat end into his left hand.

Even though they looked nervous, the two clerks brought up their bats, too.

Then they started down the stairs.

16

Hit and Run

JUPE RAISED HIS FISTS. IT LOOKED LIKE HE WOULD LOSE THIS fight, but he wouldn't take it lying down. If he could take out Purvis, they'd have half a chance. The two clerks obviously hadn't signed on for this. They were just following the head thug.

But tackling Purvis wouldn't be an easy job. He was big, and he handled the bat as if he'd used it before. He advanced confidently down the stairs, the clerks bunched behind him.

Jupe cleared his mind, just as he did at judo practice. He wanted to be open to every nuance of his opponent's movements. His breathing slowed and grew deeper. His hands opened, ready to block or grab.

Purvis and his companions were halfway down the stairs when Jupe spotted two figures in the doorway above.

"Hey, Pete," Jupe called up to them. "The guy in the lead here is the one who punched you out."

Purvis laughed. "I never thought you'd be dumb enough to try that old 'Look behind you!' trick."

While he was talking, Pete and Bob jumped the two clerks. Bob nailed his man with a backhand blow to the side of the head. The guy dropped his bat and slumped onto the steps.

Meanwhile, Pete grabbed his man's bat hand and twisted it up behind him. He plucked the bat from the surprised clerk's grasp and poked down at Purvis with it.

"This is the guy I really want to fight," he said.

Purvis made a quick recovery. With a yell he whipped around, swinging his bat straight at Pete's head. Pete parried the blow awkwardly, and his bat slammed out of his hand. The guy he'd been holding twisted free and began grappling with Bob.

Jupe jumped forward the moment Purvis was distracted. He went up three steps, but his movement alerted the big thug, who swung the bat behind him backhand.

The end of the bat whipped right in front of Jupe's face. Then it cracked into the old wooden railing. Jupe moved up another step, trying to pin the bat with one hand while grabbing for Purvis's wrist with the other.

But Purvis thudded into him with his body, trying to knock Jupe down the stairs. With a grunt of pain Jupe lost his grip. He was forced to cling to the railing to keep from falling. Purvis laughed as he pulled the bat free.

He turned again to swing at Pete and Bob, keeping them back, then went to finish Jupe.

But Jupe wasn't where he was supposed to be. He came in under Purvis's swing. Propelling himself up the staircase like a human missile, his head caught Purvis square in the gut.

Whoof! The thug folded, stumbling back into the arms of Bob and Pete. Even then he kept fighting, catching Bob in the side of the neck with a fist.

"Enough of this," Pete finally said, throwing himself on the guy. They rolled down the stairs together, with Pete landing on top.

He hauled Purvis to his feet and smiled. "You know," he said, "you've got quite a punch. What do you think of mine?"

Then he decked him.

Bob had already taken care of the second clerk. The two Kamikaze employees sat on the steps, all the fight knocked out of them.

"Wow!" Bob called down to Jupe, who was still rubbing his head. "That last move was something. Judo?"

"Stupidity." Jupe winced as his fingers touched a sensitive spot.

"Well, it worked," Pete said happily. "Why were these guys trying to get you, anyway?"

After Jupe brought them up to date, Pete said, "Fine. Do we call the cops now?"

"It's not that easy," Jupe said. "We might get these creeps jailed for assault, but we can't get Griswold."

"Why not?" Pete demanded. "He's a counterfeiter."

"A counterfeiter of *comic books,*" Steve Tresh spoke up. "That's not a criminal charge."

"But he's breaking the law!" Pete insisted.

"All they'd be able to get him on is violating some publisher's copyright," Jupe said. "And people usually don't get jailed to keep them around for civil suits like this."

"So he can skip town," DeMento said.

"Maybe even skip the country," Jupe said. "Let's ask some questions and find out just how big this scam is."

One of the scared salesclerks spilled all he knew—about how the comics were printed down in the basement and sold to unsuspecting collectors.

"They probably made a nice profit, too," Tresh said. "Black-and-white comics cost about two grand to counterfeit, and the middle range of collector's items go for about fifty bucks a pop. If they only ran off a hundred of each book, they'd make sixty percent on the deal."

"But Griswold was breaking things up, even getting rid of the press," Jupe pointed out. He looked at one salesclerk. "What was going on?"

"He had another deal going—for color books," the man said.

"Color?" Tresh said. "That costs more like twelve thousand dollars. Where was he getting it done?"

"Taiwan," a voice said from the bottom of the stairs. Purvis, now securely tied up, looked around in disgust. "Axel had some kind of deal with a crooked printer there. The books would be smuggled in as packing material for imported pottery. All of us Kamikaze guys would go into business as distributors up and down the entire coast. It would have been a sweet deal."

"Too bad it's gone sour," Jupe said.

They left the three tied up in the cellar and locked the shop. Rainey was glad to see them. She hadn't enjoyed sitting in the car in such a creepy neighborhood.

"Are you guys okay?" she asked anxiously. "I really got worried when those clerks threw me out and Bob and Pete had to break in."

"We're fine," Jupe assured her, skipping the details. "And now we have to catch Griswold before he gets away."

"How can we stop him?" Pete asked.

"There's still the robbery," Bob suggested. "Maybe we can nail Griswold for that—if we can catch him with the stolen comics."

Rainey sighed. "That sounds like a pretty big if."

◆ ◆ ◆

When they got back to the convention, the bustle and noise came almost as a shock. They had been half-expecting to find the place empty, like Kamikaze Komics.

The girl with the two-toned hair looked very unhappy. She'd been stuck with both entrance jobs—stamping hands and checking admissions. Jupe didn't have the heart to tell her that Purvis wouldn't be back to help her out.

"What now?" Bob asked as they rushed onto the convention floor.

"Find Griswold before he finds us," Pete said. "He sent that gorilla to take care of us. If he sees us scouting around, he'll know something's up."

"I agree," Jupe said. "Find Griswold. And find those comics."

"Hey, what's with you guys?" a booming voice asked. Frank the Crank Carne came barreling through the crowd. "You look excited—all in a sweat. What's up?"

Steve Tresh grabbed him by the arm. "Frank, do you know where Axel Griswold is right now?"

Carne's teeth glistened in a grin behind his beard. "Something exciting *is* up. Is it another disaster old Axel can wring his hands over?"

He laughed, but Jupe got a quick vision of Griswold coming up after the robbery—rubbing his long, thin hands together. Hands that hadn't been stamped, of course. The convention boss wouldn't need an admission ticket, especially with his stooge, Purvis, at the door.

"You know, Griswold's hands match the robber's—long fingers, and no stamp on the back," Jupe said. "I'd think he pulled the job, but two people saw him go into the Gold Room at the time of the robbery." He frowned, thinking.

"I saw him in the Gold Room then. He came in and complained that the projectionist wasn't there," Carne said. "He tried to start the projector, but he couldn't make it work. The stupid thing wasn't even adjusted for the screen. He had to use his bag to prop it up."

"Bag? What bag?" Jupe wanted to know.

Carne shrugged. "He had a canvas bag over his shoulder—like half the people at this convention."

"He didn't have a bag when we met him," Pete said.

"And that wasn't so long before the robbery," Bob added.

"More importantly, what was *in* that bag?" Jupe asked.

"You think it was the costume?" said Rainey.

"Could be." Jupe frowned again. "But the timing is off. How could he get out of the costume and into the Gold Room so quickly?"

"Good question," said Pete.

"I'd like to check out the Gold Room," Jupe announced. "C'mon."

They headed off the convention floor, made a left, and then another left down a long corridor.

"Ever notice how inconvenient they make it to get to these places?" Tresh said with a grin.

Toward the end of the hall, on the right, was the entrance to the Gold Room. Through the closed door they could hear thrilling music and a woman's voice crying, "Blast him, Rock!"

On the left was a blank door without a doorknob. Jupe pushed against it, but the door didn't budge. "Where does this lead?" he asked.

"That's an emergency exit," Carne said. "The convention's on the other side."

Jupe put his ear to the door and caught the sounds of moving bodies and hubbub on the convention floor. "You know," he said, his eyes alight, "this door would have made things very easy for the Crimson Phantom after he pulled the robbery. It's very close to Dan DeMento's stall."

"He'd have to change again," Tresh objected.

"He made his own changing room—the smoke cloud." Jupe turned to Rainey. "Tell me again what you saw when you looked back at the cloud."

She shrugged. "Just a glimpse of red flapping over the guy's shoulder as he disappeared in the smoke."

Jupe nodded. "And which way was he headed?"

Rainey paused. "Gee, I thought it was toward the front door—but it could have been to this side exit instead!"

Jupe grinned. "And the flapping robe could have been Griswold whipping off the costume to stuff it into his bag along with the stolen comics!"

"But I saw him in the Gold Room just before the robbery," Carne began.

"Right," Jupe cut in. "Just before you *heard* about the robbery."

Carne looked confused. "What do you . . . oh. I'm beginning to get what you mean."

"I don't," Pete confessed.

"It would take a couple of minutes for news of the robbery to get out the front door of the convention room and come down this hallway," Bob said.

Jupe nodded. "Right. Just by stepping out the side exit, Griswold could outrun the news and make his appearance in the Gold Room. He'd be safely in there when people started talking about the robbery. No one would suspect him.

"That leaves just one loose end," Jupe added. "The bag Griswold brought into the Gold Room. I wonder if it's still propping up the projector in there."

"We could go find out," Steve Tresh said.

"It would be better if *Griswold* went to find out," Jupe said. "Let's send him a message from the projectionist."

"My pal Hunter is in there now, running the projector," Carne interrupted. "He'll send a message. What do you want him to say?"

Jupe smiled. "How about something like, 'The projector is heating up. There's gonna be a fire!' "

17

Smoking Out a Rat

THE DOORS TO THE GOLD ROOM FLEW OPEN, THROWING A swath of light on the die-hard serial fans. Several didn't even notice—they were fast asleep. Others were too intent on the screen. But a few complained, "Hey! Close that door!"

On the screen Rock Asteroid went into his final struggle with Gung, king of the Muckmen, as thrilling music soared.

The tall figure silhouetted in the door paid no attention to the complaints or the picture. He headed straight for the projector, brushing past Hunter. Grabbing the canvas bag on the table, he started pulling it toward him. The projector shifted to one side, its beam half on, half off the screen.

All that the audience now saw was Rock raising his ray gun. His enemy disappeared.

"What's wrong with the film? What are you doing!" Even the guys who'd been asleep leaped up and began complaining. The shouting got louder when the man yanked the bag out from under the projector. The picture now dropped so the audience could see only the tops of Rock's and Gung's heads. Rock's fish-bowl helmet and Gung's antennae seemed to be dancing as the projector wobbled from side to side.

The yelling drowned out the sound track. It even drowned out the fans shouting, "Quiet! I can't hear."

Seven audience members were silent as they got up and surrounded the man by the projector—the Three Investigators, Madman Dan, Frank the Crank, Steve Tresh, and Rainey Fields. Even with the flickering light the man in the middle was unmistakable—Axel Griswold.

He stood for a moment with the bag clutched in his hands. Then he shrugged and opened it—to take out a tiny ball.

"Hold it!" Jupe shouted, but the ball had already hit the floor.

Dense smoke rose up and Griswold screamed "Fire!"

The real fans didn't even notice. They were busy making Hunter get the picture right—something that got harder and harder as smoke filled the room. Less true-blue fans bolted for the door, jostling Jupe's group apart. Griswold took his chance and charged Rainey, swinging the bag over his head.

She staggered, and he got past her, tearing his way through the still-open doors.

Jupe caught Rainey around the waist, steadying her. "Come on!" he yelled to the others.

They piled through the door to find Griswold

halfway down the hall. He was running full out, brushing people out of his way. As the Investigators plunged after him they saw Griswold straight-arm a fan. The kid went spinning away.

Griswold hit the lobby and kept straight on, jostling past people. He wasn't aiming for the front entrance or the crowd in front of the elevators.

Then Jupe realized. "The stairs! He's going for the fire stairs." Pete took the lead, gaining on Griswold's broken-field run through the lobby crowd.

Griswold skidded around a corner, and they heard the familiar clang of the fire door slamming.

Pete yanked the door open, and then they were all pelting down the stairs to the parking garage. "Go for your cars, not Griswold," Jupe yelled from his place in the middle of the pack. He remembered how DeMento had almost run them down the last time.

Sound strategy. As they came through the door Griswold was already jumping into a bright red Corvette.

The Investigators ran for the Impala. But by the time Pete got it going, the Corvette had whipped through a tight U-turn and was barreling toward the exit ramp. Pete hit the gas and sped after it.

"If this guy gets on the open road, we've had it," he said. "We'll be eating his dust."

But how were they going to stop him? Griswold had a clear path to the ramp.

Then, wheels screaming, DeMento's dark-green

van came careening from behind a pillar. It roared to cut Griswold off.

The Corvette sped up, swerving to avoid DeMento. It nosed its way past, but DeMento's van rammed into the right rear fender.

Griswold fishtailed up the ramp, the crumpled metal on the back of his car screeching.

The green van had a few more dents now. But it lurched through a wide turn up the ramp, staying right on Griswold's tail. Pete and the Investigators now brought up the rear.

Out on Century Boulevard, the Corvette sped up. But it began to shake wildly as it wove through traffic. The Investigators could hear the squeal of tortured rubber. Apparently that fender bender had been more serious than it looked. The dented metal was pressed against the tire.

Griswold couldn't leave them in the dust—too much speed, and he'd lose control of the car. They had a chance!

DeMento stayed behind Griswold, ignoring the protests of the other drivers, keeping the pressure on. Pete started jockeying across the three lanes, trying to get around and cut the Corvette off.

Griswold kept trying to accelerate, but the shaking of his car slowed him down. He just couldn't pull far enough ahead. Several times DeMento thumped into his rear bumper, shaking him up some more.

Even so, they couldn't force him off the road. Griswold kept cutting back and forth, successfully blocking any attempt to pass him. DeMento almost passed him on the left, but Griswold turned into him, putting some dents on the left side of his car.

Cars behind them were blowing their horns, startled by the strange spectacle on the road.

"You know," Bob said, "that Corvette would look more at home in a salvage yard, Jupe."

He was right. Griswold's once magnificent sports car had bashes on both sides, and the bumper had fallen off on one side. Showers of sparks flew as metal screeched against pavement. And that tire was still sending off a shrill protest as it scraped against the ruined fender.

Finally the rubber could stand no more. The tire burst, sending the Corvette veering into the oncoming traffic. Amid the squeal of brakes and a chorus of angry horns, Griswold got control of his machine.

And to his right, Dan DeMento's green van pulled ahead of him, with the Investigators maneuvering to box him in on the left.

Griswold had nothing to lose. His car shuddered wildly as he squeezed between his two pursuers, intending to cross two lanes of traffic and make the next right. DeMento swerved to cut him off.

The Corvette jockeyed for position, coming up dead behind the van.

Then the van's rear doors swung out to reveal Rainey Fields standing in the opening. She looked scared but determined, holding her cape in her hands like a bullfighter. When Griswold tried to swerve past again, she tossed the cape—right onto his windshield.

Griswold missed his turn—but he didn't miss the streetlight just beyond. *Crunch!*

When the cops arrived, they found the pursuers pinning down a groggy but unharmed Griswold. And the bag of loot was still in his hand.

18

Business As Usual

GRISWOLD WAS IN JAIL, ARRESTED FOR THEFT. BUT THE convention had its final day to run. Sunday it was more crowded than ever. The Kamikaze Komics booth was empty, but the other dealers were doing great business.

The crowd was packed around Madman Dan's stall, drawn there by the publicity of his crime-busting exploit. He had extra assistants working behind the tables, and had even been asked for a couple of autographs.

He was engaged in serious business right now, examining a set of comics for sale. "Well, they could be in better condition," he said. "A couple of pages are bent, and this cover is going to come off if you look at it hard. You should have taken better care of them—and not thrown them in my face." He grinned at Jupe.

"It seemed necessary at the time," Jupe said, grinning back. "There was a maiden in distress."

DeMento started counting out twenty-dollar bills. "We agreed on a price if you found the thief," he said, squaring up the pile of money. Then he added more bills. "We'll call this a bonus."

Jupe, Bob, and Pete couldn't believe it. Their investment had paid off handsomely—almost eight hundred bucks!

Jupe put the money in his pocket. "That's really generous of you, Dan."

"Generous, nothing. I'll make it up in fifteen minutes' worth of business," Madman Dan said. "Either that or I'll add it on to the price of *Fan Fun* when it comes back from being evidence. That thing is a *real* collector's item now—the famous phony stolen comic with the famous artist's forged autograph. I may even try to get Steve to sign a real autograph on it."

"Don't push your luck, pal. Be happy I'm signing this other stuff." Steve Tresh was inside the stall, scribbling away with his pen on a stack of comics. "If I autograph that thing, you've got to guarantee me a percentage of the profits."

"These comic people." DeMento sighed. "They all turn into businessmen."

"Except for Frank Carne," Jupe said. "Where is he?"

Tresh laughed. "Where else? In the Gold Room catching another favorite part of *Rock Asteroid*. They finally found something else to hold up the projector."

"Griswold really picked some hiding place," Bob said. "What's going to happen now that his little racket's been exposed?"

"Dealers and collectors from San Diego to Frisco are tearing their hair." DeMento shook his head. "They're not happy to discover that the black-and-whites they bought from Griswold are fakes instead of the bargains they thought they were."

Tresh looked grim. "The scary thing is, he could have kept it up forever if he hadn't gone overboard with that autograph trick. But he went for the bigger money, forging people's signatures onto his phony books to jack up the prices."

"I've heard people moaning about how he took them," Pete said. "He'd show the mark a counterfeit, tell them he'd just picked it up, and ask what they thought about it. They'd discover the autograph, and since Griswold hadn't mentioned *that*, they'd think he hadn't noticed it and snap the book up."

"Their greed was Griswold's gain," Jupe said. "He took a lot of people—even Leo Rottweiler. Then he made his mistake, inviting Steve to the convention—before finding out that Rottweiler had sold his autographed *Fan Fun*."

Tresh nodded. "He figured if I saw the book, it would blow his whole scam."

"Leo sure was in a sweat to buy the book back!" DeMento grinned.

"But you wouldn't sell—so Griswold dressed up as the Crimson Phantom and stole the book," Jupe continued. "That was followed by a campaign to get Tresh out of the convention. Griswold didn't want Steve finding out about the forged autograph. He

was afraid his whole ...
ravel."

"He didn't know I had other business here," Tresh said.

"And he encouraged Jupe, Pete, and me so he'd look innocent," Bob added. "He figured we'd be easy enough to fool."

"And from our inept start, we sure gave him hope," Jupe admitted. "He planted those comics in Rainey's bag to keep us totally confused."

Pete laughed. "But we nailed him in the end, didn't we?"

"We did—with a lot of help," Jupe said. "Thanks, guys."

"Yeah. Well, if you want to sell the rest of whatever you found in that trunk full of comics, come by the shop someday. I'll see if I can arrange some deals." DeMento waved good-bye.

"Just don't ask for any autographs." Tresh grinned.

The Investigators were headed for the entrance to the hall when they saw camera flashes. There was Rainey Fields, enjoying her new-found celebrity. The media people were all over her—the all-American girl who nabbed a crook superstyle.

"Jupe!" Her face lit up when she saw him.

"Um—hi," he said.

"The silver tongue strikes again," Bob muttered behind him.

Rainey didn't notice. She's looking at me, Jupe realized. *Me!*

of guy!"

Rainey." Jupe glanced at him and lowered his voice a little. Maybe after all this is over, we can get together. Where do you live?"

"Um. Portland."

Jupe blinked. "You mean Portland as in Oregon?"

"Yup." Rainey nodded.

"Well, it's a longer drive than I was expecting, but . . ."

"You nut!" Rainey began laughing. "But I hope we *will* get some time to see each other. If I get some modeling jobs in L.A., for instance."

"Or if I get up to Portland." Jupe sighed.

"Don't look *so* sad," Rainey said with a grin. "There's still the convention here. We've got a whole day to enjoy . . ."

Jupe found himself grinning back. "Guys, I'll see you later."

"What about our money?" Pete and Bob wanted to know.

Jupe handed over their shares. "I just found a use for mine," he said with a big smile. "I'm going to spend it on a Rainey day."